Sparrow's Well

Anna Marie Savino

For The Figure:
You have my heart.

For Sparrow, my heart:
I put you through so much as I lived and wrote this part of our story.

For my readers:
Welcome to my journey.
May you be inspired to seek and find treasures that await you on
your own journey.

Table of Contents

Preface 7

At First: No Well 11

The Door 15

The Court Yard 29

The Mere Ore Forest 43

Swamped 63

The Secret Cave 81

Bull's "I" 99

Waking Up 113

It Is Well 129

Afterward 141

Acknowledgements 143

About the Storyteller 145

Preface

Most of my life, I have felt underestimated and misunderstood. It is now obvious to me why I chose a profession that includes guiding people to both understand others and be understood by others through interacting with each other's stories.

All our stories begin and end with The Word, which might just be the most underrated, powerful, and multifaceted tool we possess to build a better world. The Word can plant a seed that, when nourished with water and light, sprouts into ideas, that then bloom into actions, that in effect become the fruitful nature of Life. The Word is what gives Life meaning.

The pages in this book contain multiple words that illustrate a fantastical account of a very realistic journey through healing my heart. Since all the words I write and speak and think are rooted in my heart, I need to make sure that my heart is well-nourished. I want my words to be nurturing, not poisonous. Being someone who has hurt and been hurt with words, I understand their power. My well-intentioned purpose for using words is to bring healing.

Sharing our stories, fictional or not, is what shapes our morals, values, and actions. Narrative is such a powerful tool that can enhance personal growth. The beauty about sharing one's own story and reading others' personal narratives is that, if we take time to learn about the details of each other's small parts, we can all learn about the bigger story: The One in which we are *all* participating.

We all have a story to tell, yet our stories are not completely our own. Because the themes in our own lives often match the themes in the lives of others, when we share parts of our story, it can resonate personally with those who hear or read it. That is exactly my goal in sharing this part of my story with you.

I have invited parts of others' stories into this story through many allusions. I play with language the way some play with video games and toys. I use puns and metaphors the way that Emeril uses spices. My intention for doing this is to concoct a well-seasoned blend of my experience and what others have brought to The Table in the One Verse we all share together. I hope that you savor the feast of words that has been prepared for you.

Although the setting and some of the characters of this story are obviously fictitious, all that I share is a real part of how I ventured into deep places within myself. I visualized the landscape and inhabitants of my mind and heart. Some of the places are beautiful, while others are horrifying. It can be a scary place: Inside. It is where I met The Emotions and the most important Character in this story. Through spending quality time with them, they transformed into internal guides who help me navigate the landscape of Inside and manage the way I perceive and interact with Outside.

I spent much of my life grabbing onto the tangible of Outside: possessions I thought I would always have if I could keep a tight enough grasp on them. The mental tug-of-war between holding on and letting go is tedious and exhausting. Regardless of the outcome, something is always lost, and something is always gained. Usually, I focused more on the loss than on the victory.

Being able to see through the lens of victory takes time and effort. Venturing on a variety of paths that lead to identifying and attempting to nurture my needs both Inside and Outside has taken a long time, but I have learned to be more patient with the process and the progress. I still struggle on my journey and probably will until I literally reach the Other Side.

It is so difficult to say goodbye to things that I think keep me safe and happy on this Side but turn out to be the very daggers that cause my wounds. Letting go was the only way to stop hurting myself so that I could heal. It took me a long time and so much effort to finally let go. Now, I know that it is possible. Now, I know that I am capable. Now, I know that it is important for me to share that part of my journey with you.

Through my journey, I learned that I cannot fully enjoy anything if I don't consistently let everything have the freedom to be what it is. I also learned that the more I try to hold onto something and control it, the more I destroy what I loved about it in the first place. An open hand can more thoroughly and lovingly experience what it holds. We may hold things such as relationships, jobs, memories, hopes, and beliefs. I have learned that these things are better out of our tightly clenched fists.

It has been said that one bird in the hand is worth two in the bush. Through my journey, I have learned that I don't want to possess or hold any birds. I just want to hear them sing and watch them fly freely. If one wants to land on my finger to perch for a while, I will welcome it openly. It is always free to fly away. My hands will never again be a cage for anything that comes my way.

Just like birds, our hearts should not be in cages. Yes, out of the cage, they are more vulnerable; but, just as birds were made to fly, a heart yearns to be free to explore and share in exchange for that which nourishes it to grow. We imprison our hearts when we keep them in cages, and we wonder why we feel unsatisfied in this life. Freeing my heart was unnerving, but it was the only way I could truly learn to live and let live in the most sustainably satisfying relationship I have ever known.

The purpose of sharing my story is not as much for you to get to know *me*, rather it is for you to connect with and use my story to get to know your own story better. This journey was written with the initial intention to be narrative therapy for me. My goal for sharing it is to communicate my experience and inspire you to take from it what you will and make it your own. By the end of this story, I hope you find more treasures in your own journey after reading about those in mine.

At First: No Well

Darkness crept into the forest and a thunderous sound filled the once calm and quiet air. The stone façade of The Well crumbled and buried a frail bird who was simply quenching its thirst in the murky, yet readily available, water Inside.

Cracked and shattered stones lay on top of each other, sprinkled with soft dust, at the place where The Well once stood. A shadow unfolded over the pile of rubble, like a blanket covering the newly deceased. A yellow swallowtail butterfly landed on the pile just long enough for me to see that it had a broken right wing. Then, it flew upwards toward a cluster of ominous clouds that darkened the sky and threatened rain.

Parched with my empty cup, I stood paralyzed staring at the broken stones at my feet. I could hear a faint voice singing from deep within the debris, and the melody unchained me into action. I dropped my cup and bent down to try to lift the stones off to save whatever was trapped, but I had no strength. As I let go of my attempt to save the creature attached to that helpless voice, tears welled up in my eyes. The heavy clouds must have empathized, as they, too, began to weep.

The bucket-like lump in my throat made its way down into my heart, carried the salty water to my eyes, and dumped it down my cheeks. As each drop fell into the now muddied dust, I could clearly see that the tears contained memories of everything that had happened before the moment The Well crumbled. I saw memories pass away before my eyes as they fell onto the ground and were buried.

Although I felt as dry as a desert, my eyes continued to leak memory-filled droplets of water; each tear contributing to the delusional ocean of amnesia that started to drown me in my own thirst.

With whetted eyes, I picked up my empty cup, looked up at the dark sky, and wished to fly beyond the clouds into the sunshine that I knew existed above the weeping shadows in front of me, separating and guarding me from the untouchable Universe. Staring into the vastness, I wondered how I was going to escape this situation; I wondered how long it would take to run to one of the stars or the sun; I wondered why my problems seemed so big, when they were actually miniscule compared to the infinite space around me.

My wonderings took the form of questions; *"What is the Universe? Why is it so infinite; so untouchable; so distant; so unattainable?"*

My neck began to tighten as I continued to look upwards, seeing a bridge between the infinite and the finite. The questions continued. *"Why do we feel hurt or pain? Is love the remedy to hurt or pain? What is the point of love? Is love the opposite of fear? Why do I have so much fear? Where do all of these feelings and experiences come from and, more importantly, where do they go when they are finished?"*

My gaze left the sky and landed back on the dust-covered fragments on the ground. I realized, *"That is where we all go. Ashes to ashes; dust to dust. Just like my memories fell from my tears and buried themselves in the ground, everything I do while I am here will get buried with me, and then what? If we have come from nowhere and go to nowhere when this is all over, what is the point of anything we do while we are here?"*

There has to be a logical explanation for why we are here and why our experiences are attached to feelings ranging between extreme bliss and pain; I was determined to figure out the answers to the questions. I was no longer just thirsty for water; I was also deeply parched for understanding.

At the moment of that realization, I saw a figure illuminated in the distance. It drew my attention away from the clouds and shadows.

My body trembled as I tried to figure out the mirage.

It is a lion?

No, It looks more like a human.

It isn't even moving! It must be a giant rock.

No, look at the way a mane blows in the wind! It is a lion.

No, wait! That is a robe blowing in the wind! It is a human! I can see hands stretched out, welcoming an embrace.

The ambiguity of the illusion was disturbing enough, but I *truly* began to panic when The Figure became larger and clearer. It progressed toward me quickly, Its feet hit the ground in the rhythm of a deliberate knock.

I wondered if It was dangerous. The knocking became louder. Terror pulsed up and down my spine as I ran twelve steps away from the cold pile of stones. Although it was only a short distance, I felt like I had run harder and faster than I ever had before. I felt suffocated by the rapidly frightening experience. Breathing was difficult. My body was so exhausted that I collapsed, just as The Well did earlier. While I was grounded, I decided to rest. I fell asleep for a long time in the dust.

The Door

I had no idea how long I was asleep. I awoke covered in dirt with my hands curled into fists, prepared to fight. My hands were clenched so tightly that my fingernails drew blood in crescent-moon shapes in the flesh of my hands. Opening my palms and seeing the red stained nail marks in the middle made me realize that my fight was between letting go and holding on so tightly to things; to control; to the fight itself.

I could vaguely see the pile of broken well stones approximately twelve steps away from me. The Figure that terrified me was standing over the stones.

The moment my eyes saw The Figure, a cacophonous outburst of shouting filled the air. From a distance, I could see silhouettes of trees coming to life. They ripped themselves out of the ground, using the emerged, gangly roots to propel themselves toward me. Each one picked up a broken stone from the remains of The Well with their branches. Once the ends of the branches had a stone secured, it was aimed in my direction.

With blurred vision, I turned my eyes toward the place where The Figure was now kneeling on the ground.

The Figure did not move. With Its glance fixed in my direction, I found myself drawn toward It. The trees broke my concentration on The Figure by screaming at me while their limbs were still pulled back in anticipation of hurling stones directly at me. Something immediately stopped their progression.

The Figure brushed aside the sticks scattered on the ground and started writing in the dust with a stone. I could not see what

The Figure was writing, but some of the trees dropped their stones upon seeing what was written. The more The Figure wrote, the more trees dropped their stones.

Curiosity moved me toward the trees. As I moved closer, I heard a whisper. "Wait!"

The Word paralyzed me.

The Figure kept writing until all the trees surrendered their stones. After the last stone was released to the ground, The Figure arose before me. I felt like falling to my knees in gratitude.

"What just happened?" I asked, astonished, feeling like I needed to look away in embarrassment. However, I could not take my eyes off what was before me. I was stunned by my ambiguous attraction to The Figure. My eyes were fixated on It for a long time while the rest of the surroundings of the forest became hazy and dim.

Then, The Figure began to speak to me. "I AM here to help you, if you want My help."

"Why do I need Your help?" I asked.

"You'll see," was all The Figure replied with a confident smirk. I was frustrated with that answer.

"What are You doing here? Where did You come from?" I had so many questions.

"All of the details that you need to know will be revealed in the time that you will understand them. For now, you are ready to learn about what I have been waiting to share with you since the day you were knit together in your mother's womb. It has taken you a long time to grow into this moment. There is so much that I want to share with you, Anna."

The Figure spoke so strangely, and It knew my name! My curiosity was piqued. "Who are You?" I asked.

16

"You have known My Name, but you have not known who I AM, Anna."

"I don't understand," I said, absolutely confused. "Why are You here, and how am I going to quench my thirst now that The Well is broken?"

"The Well has always been a place for nourishment, but it has also represented transformation. People who have been to The Well before you experienced your same troubles. I have seen it many times in this forest. I met a woman a long time ago here at The Well. My companions and I were heading North, just as I was doing today. It was a detour from the way we were supposed to go, but I had a very important appointment with her at The Well. It is very similar to what happened today. I had an appointment with you, and here I AM."

"*You* had an appointment with *me*? I came here for water because I was so thirsty. I was incredibly disappointed that, when I got here, The Well was destroyed. I am still very thirsty."

"I would like to continue to share the story about My appointment. It is a beautiful story!" It was as if The Figure didn't hear that I said I was thirsty.

"Is there any way that we can get something to drink first?"

"We will need to walk together for a little while in order to quench your thirst. Shall we walk and talk?"

I nodded in agreement.

The Figure began to tell me stories about one of Its ancestors *and* the woman who It met at The Well. Both found conflict and treasure at The Well- each at separate times in the history of the forest. The Figure also told me that my story is an extension of both of their stories; and of Its own story: that all stories are One.

"It is the secret of the Uni...Verse." The Figure said the two parts of the word *universe* in deliberately separated terms. "Not everyone comes to The Well, but everyone has the opportunity. Those who do find treasures, not just here in the forest, but also beyond the trees. Everyone has the opportunity to live outside of the forest, but many are so comfortable here, that they cannot imagine what is beyond the security of what they know here."

Since I didn't know what The Figure was talking about when It mentioned 'a life beyond security,' I asked many questions. "So, what do I do now that The Well is gone? How do *I* fit into the One story? How do I find what is beyond the forest; isn't that only 'a place I heard of once in a lullaby'?"

"*Somewhere* like that, yes. I am happy to take you there. Do you think you can *trust* Me to show you?"

The Figure's question both terrified and comforted me.

I looked around the forest. My eyes met the debris of the crumbled well. I admitted- for the first time, "I don't know if I am capable of *trusting*."

"Well, you are talking to Me as we walk together right now. You don't really know Me, but you are asking Me questions. That is one form of *trust*."

Surprised by that answer, I paused for a moment to reflect. I never thought that I had any trust. I want to trust, but I quickly find that I have expectations that nothing or no one can really meet. The few times I have given into trust, I learned that it wasn't safe to do so. Since then, I have been keeping my heart safe from predators. There are many, and I have met quite a few of them. I feel as though I have nothing left to give because of my experiences with them.

"If you only focus on what you *don't* have, you will tend to forget that there are little things you do every day that require some form of trust. There is still a spark of trust left within you that has not been extinguished," The Figure said to me, as if It knew more about me than I did. The dwindling heat from that spark The Figure mentioned inflamed and started to warm my heart.

We must have been in earshot of The Well because I remember, at that moment I felt the warmth, I heard a faint singing coming from the pile of stones. The song must have been coming from whatever was trapped inside. "I hear it again! I heard it just after The Well Crumbled! We need to go back and rescue it!"

"What is it?" The Figure asked, seeming to already know the answer.

"Something became trapped in The Well after it crumbled. I remember hearing its voice inside The Well."

"I see," chuckled The Figure. "Well, what if I told you that it is safe as it happily sings right now?"

"Happy and safe while crumbled inside The Well?" I was incredulous.

"Even though some people see a bird as worth half a penny, I know when one is hurt or has passed away in my forest. I know every creature here, and I know that a bird, although stuck, is safe. In order to save it, we need to keep walking in this direction." When The Figure pointed North, light from the sun reflected through Its hand and shone on a path ahead of us.

Confused by Its response, I asked, "Why can't You just give me straight-forward answers?"

"What fun would that be?" The Figure answered.

I had a feeling that I was in for an interesting experience

with The Figure and Its strange answers and appointments and adventures. "Where does that path lead?" I inquired.

"It leads to *The Door*."

I trembled. "You mean *The Door* that I have heard so many people talk about for so long and have seen pictures of since I was a child? *The Door* that has caused so many wars and battles here in the forest?"

"Yes. It leads to *The Door*. I want to show it to you. Do you *trust* Me to take you there?"

I hesitated. The Well had crumbled. I was so thirsty. I had nothing to lose at this point, so I looked up at The Figure and answered, "I don't know if I *trust* You yet, but I will go with You."

The Figure smiled.

We walked together in silence until we reached *The Door*, which was one of the most carefully constructed pieces of work I had ever seen. It contained many panels with either a story, or a poem, or a historical event of high significance carved into pictures. Each panel was separated into smaller sections that were numbered, so that people in the forest could more easily reference and discuss which section of the panel they want to describe when they shared about what they saw. *The Door* stood eleven rows of panels high with six panels across each row. It was very apparent that High Intelligence was involved in the design of *The Door*. The detail and construction that went into each panel was that of a very skilled Carpenter and Master Craftsman who worked with the help of authors, poets, and historians.

I heard about *The Door* before. I saw pictures of it and listened to others talk about it. However, everyone seemed to have their own interpretation of it. When The Figure led me to

The Door, I saw that many people's descriptions of *The Door* only came from small parts of it! I understood why. It is a massive creation to describe with so many little intricacies that make up its composition.

Surrounding *The Door* were vines, some with thorns and dried-up leaves. Seeing the dryness reminded me how thirsty I was.

"What do we do now that we are here?" I asked, overwhelmed by the enormity of what was before me.

"In order to quench your thirst, we must contemplate the panels together. Tell me what you see in that first panel," The Figure said as It looked up at the first panel with the pride of an artist displaying work.

"I see a poem at the top."

"Will you read it to Me?"

Before I could utter the first word of the poem, I heard loud trumpets blaring powerfully, as if to indicate that a king was nearby. At first, the sound scared me, and I backed away from *The Door*. Then, I looked at the smile of The Figure as It waved Its hands to mimic a conductor. It nodded Its head at me and looked back up to the first panel with a gleam of contentment and anticipation of my reading.

I turned back to face *The Door* and focused on the first words. As I read, the words come out as a song. I had heard the words before, but never as a song. I was taken aback, as I understood the lyrics well, and yet, I never encountered the melody before standing right in front of *The Door* with The Figure by my side.

The first two parts of The Song were intricately creative! The ending of the first two parts of The Song was *so* good!

Then, the melody began to change during the third part of The Song. The major harmony of the beginning darkened into minor cacophony. It rumbled like an earthquake in my heart, and I began to feel sick. The Song was no longer pleasant.

"This is where The Emotions began to determine experiences, Anna. This is where you find out how The Well crumbled."

I didn't like that. I was upset. "The beginning of The Song was so beautiful! Why did it change?"

"This is what your journey with Me will help you understand. I won't simply tell you. You wouldn't understand. I will teach you as we go, but you must take the journey."

"You are a teacher?"

"In one way, yes."

"Can You teach me about The Song, *The Door,* and The Well?"

"Listen to the way the forest reveals The Song, look at what you see in *The Door,* and wait for The Well to be restored to understand."

"The Well will be restored?"

"Yes. If you want it to be."

"Of course! I want The Well to be restored."

"You will need to be disciplined, Anna. I know that you love running around the forest, enjoying its beauty and making friends. All of that is fine. I am glad that you enjoy it here. If you want to restore The Well, understand *The Door,* and learn more about The Song, you and I need to spend time here, together. I will be your Teacher, and you would be My pupil. I will show you the forest through My eyes, and you will understand all that you seek to understand. It will take time and effort. Nothing worthwhile in the forest comes easily. There is much you will need to leave behind, but I promise that what you will gain will be worth much, much more. The journey will be frustrating at times. There will be times when it will even be painful, but I can promise you that it will be worth it in the end. Are you ready for that kind of discipline?"

The task seemed daunting. I loved playing in the forest. Everyday brought new adventures and new ideas to learn. I would need to put all other adventures on hold in order to embark on this new adventure with The Figure. Was I willing to give that up just to sit in front of *The Door*? What if I don't succeed in learning The Song? So many questions flooded my mind again.

I turned to The Figure and asked, "What do I need to do to progress?"

"Keep looking at the first panel of *The Door*," guided The Figure. This is where your story begins and My story continues.

"Just looking at it makes me dizzy and tired," I was still debating if I wanted to begin the journey or not.

"It takes a special kind of strength that people are not necessarily encouraged to build upon while they are here. It is easier to hear about *The Door* from someone else. The strength comes from continually being here at *The Door* and fighting the danger that lurks around it."

"What danger is around it?"

"You'll see," was all The Figure said. "For now, look at *The Door* and see how it is relevant to all you have experienced so far. So many people do not take time to make connections between *The Door* and their own experience. They claim *The Door* is ancient and thus no longer relevant."

"How do I find the relevancy of *The Door*?" I asked.

"That is a very important question for you to ask, but it is a very difficult one to answer right now. What I can tell you is this: part of your journey is to understand *The Door* and share it with others in a way that is more relevant and accessible to them. That is the purpose of your journey. You will share this experience with others so that they can see *The Door* in a different light. It is not necessarily the way that everyone will see it, and not all of those with whom you share will listen to you. In fact, some people may hate you for sharing your experience here. There will always be people like that. However, there are some people who will never travel to *The Door* on their own if they do not hear about your experience. They will spend their lives believing lies about *The Door* if you do not encourage them to come here and observe it for themselves."

"I don't really understand," I admitted. I wanted to understand, but the thought of looking at all the panels for myself and telling others about *The Door* did not sound like what I wanted to spend my time doing. There were so many other exciting adventures. I began to resent that I agreed to come to *The Door* with The Figure. I was now given a responsibility that I did not know if I wanted. *"Why did I agree to come to The Door in the first place?"* I wondered.

Reading my mind, The Figure replied, "You were thirsty, Anna," and gently motioned to the empty cup in my hand. "First things first. Look at this panel." The Figure pointed to the middle section of *The Door*. "It is in the fourth section of the forty-third panel. This will be one of the most important sections for you right now. Look at it and tell Me what you see."

I looked at the panel. I saw a woman and a well. She looked

ashamed at first, but then, after looking deeper into her story on the forty-third panel, I saw something that resembled The Figure! "Is that You?" I asked.

"Yes. I AM in that panel. I AM in many of them. You could almost say that I AM in all of them!" The Figure chuckled a bit again, smiled, and looked at *The Door* from top to bottom. I didn't know if what The Figure said was a joke or if it was true. I think The Figure understood my incredulity based on my squinted eyes and wrinkled brow.

"Here," The Figure extended Its arm all the way and pointed up, "look at the first panel again."

When I looked at the first panel, I saw that The Well was also in the 29th section. This was the section about one of The Figure's ancestors. I looked through the entire section. I heard about this section before, but seeing it for myself made it much more personal! There is a beautiful story about love, karma, and finding *trust* represented in that section that began at The Well. I knew why The Figure pointed it out to me.

"The Well in both of those stories is the same Well. How can that be? It looks like many years passed between these two stories!"

"All stories are One." The Figure had said this before, and it seemed to be true because this story reminded me so much of my own.

"How can it be that something that happened so long ago could be so relevant to me?"

"It all is relevant. You will come to find out that everything you see in each of these panels on *The Door* is, in an intimate way, relevant to you."

"Is it relevant to everyone or just me?"

"Everyone who lives in the forest has a chance to find relevance in *The Door*. Not many people like to spend time here because it is a dangerous place to be. It also is quite daunting for those who cannot be still long enough to sit with *The Door* and look at all the panels and sections. Many people in the forest talk about *some* of the details of the panels, but to see it all together as One Story--One Verse-- is what makes sense out of each of the individual details. If people are confused about the meaning in any individual section, all they need to do is look at *all* of the sections and panels of *The Door* and see that they are all One," The Figure said to me while gesturing a request for my cup. I reluctantly handed the empty cup to The Figure. It was a test of trust. At that point, I figured, *What did I have to lose?*

Something rustled the bushes at the base of the trees around us. I looked in the direction from where the sound came, and saw something peeking out from behind a tree. It shook its head at me and then disappeared.

I looked at The Figure. "What was that all about?" I asked.

"That was the enemy," said The Figure.

"The enemy? Why? What did it want?"

"It overheard us talking and knows the value of that cup. Although it is thirstier than you are, it will never be able to drink what I AM giving you now." The Figure filled the cup and handed it back to me. "Every time I attempt to quench someone's thirst, it lurks close by to try to steal the cup."

A low-pitched shriek interrupted The Figure's advice. The branches of the trees where the enemy lurked rustled and shook. The trees looked like they were trembling with fright. I could hear hooves galloping away from *The Door*.

"Be mindful of where you choose to fill your cup. There are those in the forest that you cannot trust. However, don't let that keep you from trusting those whom you can and should trust to guide you," instructed The Figure, as It filled my cup again and guided me to look at more of the panels.

We looked at the twenty-third section of the nineteenth panel. It was one of the most beautiful poems I read on that panel. I spent much time at that panel until I understood the relevancy. As I pondered the panel, I took more sips from my cup. My mind became full, and my body became tired.

"Here," The Figure invited me to lay on a patch of green pasture. "Rest for a while."

I fell asleep once again. This time, I was content and refreshed.

The Court Yard

I awoke to warmth penetrating my cold arms. When I opened my eyes, I could see that the beams of light that pierced down on my body were coming from The Sun. It was morning, and The Figure was still with me.

"Good morning, Anna. Are you ready for your adventure today?"

"Are we going to stay here at *The Door* so I can learn more about the stories, songs, and poems in the panels?" I asked in a half-dream-like state-of-mind.

"We will come back to *The Door* soon. You can't take it all in at one time. Many times, people look at one or two panels and then walk in the forest for a while. It helps to better understand the panels if you see evidence of them in the reality of the forest." The Figure paused and switched dispositions. "You have an appointment today that will help you make more sense out of what you see in the panels."

"*An appointment?*" I was confused. "*What kind of appointment?*" I was nervous to go into anything blindly.

"You'll see," The Figure said with a smile. "All answers will be revealed to you when it is time."

I stayed silent for a while after I heard that because my mind was so loud. Ideas and questions bounced around, strategically aimless inside of my head. They either purposefully tried to cause confusion or desperately tried to find a way out without knowing how. Sometimes, I wish I could make the questions stop, but it seems as though the momentum of the questions propels me into adventures such as this.

The Figure interrupted my cacophonous silence by pointing at a large, iron gate that was attached to a highly stacked stone wall.

"That is where you need to go first, Anna."

"Are You going with me?"

"All you need to do is invite Me, and I will go with you."

"Why do You need an invitation?"

"I want to be invited. True intimacy is always summoned by special invitation and is never forced."

Intimacy? I never thought about *intimacy* with The Figure. We shared some meaningful moments at *The Door*, but was I ready for *intimacy*? At this point, The Word actually frightened me.

I never knew full-fledged intimacy, as the majority of my "intimate" relationships had at least one or two or three million impenetrable barriers. Some barriers come in the form of physical distance, others come in the form of emotional unavailability or wrong-timing or too-many-boxes-left-unchecked. It is difficult to break through the walls of others, but it almost feels impossible to break through my own walls. I work so hard to "say the right things" and "do the right things" that I create many of those barriers on my own side while trying to protect my vulnerability and authenticity.

I immediately impose an imitation-intimacy in my relationships. Within the walls I build to protect myself, I imprison the very things that invite genuine intimacy. Instead of inviting someone into the spaces of myself that would evoke a deep intimacy, I flirt with the ideas of intimacy and then erect a wall as soon as I get too close.

Maybe that is why I was still alone. I needed to break down the barriers instead of building them. I needed to learn to be inviting.

"What would it look like for me to be more inviting? What would I need to do to open up to true intimacy?" I asked feeling the scramble of more questions crashing the rowdy question-party in my mind.

"If we go in there," The Figure pointed to the gate, "it is inevitable that you will understand what you need to do to knock down your walls and open up to intimacy. As a result, *we* will become more intimate."

My curiosity was piqued, and more than ever, the questions were tantruming to escape and find their answer. As if propelled by the questions, my feet floated effortlessly forward toward the iron bars. The Figure stood still, far behind me, as I progressed closer to the gate. The closer I got, the colder the air around me became. I felt the wind slithering through my hair. Something about entering that gate began to frighten me. I looked back at The Figure and heard commotion from Inside.

"Please join me. I don't want to go in there alone."

"You are never alone, Anna. Lonely, maybe, but never alone," The Figure said while walking toward me.

I pushed on the ice-cold bars. It opened easily, and we moved together past the iron, snake-like figures of the gate that guarded whatever awaited us.

Upon entering, I saw the gate and brick wall were protecting a garden. There were flowers everywhere. The red, yellow, and pink freesia and white chrysanthemums were vibrantly alive and fragrant. The brightness of each color was illuminated by rays of sunshine. As the flowers swayed in the cool breeze, I could hear the rustling of dried leaves. Following the sound, my gaze toward the beauty was diverted to a section of the garden where monarchs fluttered above droopy delphinium, cacti, and debris of daisies that covered an area resembling an unkempt graveyard.

As I took in the sights before me, another flush of wind flurried over my skin, causing the hairs on my arm to stand at attention. I shivered down to my core. The sun was shining, and I knew that it wasn't cold outside. The oxymoronic atmosphere invited me into a deep pensiveness. I realized that my coldness was coming from Inside. I began to shake. The Figure noticed.

"Walk with Me, Anna," The Figure whispered and then motioned with Its hand for us to continue deeper into the garden. Not wanting to be alone, I instinctively grabbed The Figure's hand and held it tightly. I could feel something different in Its hand, as if that hand had been severely wounded.

"What happened to Your hand?" I asked.

"Love," The Figure replied.

"Love? How?"

"You'll see," was all The Figure said. "For now, you need to pay attention to this garden."

We walked quietly together on the paved paths that separated each bed of flowers. It was nice to share in the beauty of the dew on the roses, and I was thankful to have the comfort of The Figure's hand while we walked through the bedraggled sections.

"What is this place?" I asked.

Before The Figure answered, I heard, "She's here! Finally! She is here!" in a loud voice that shrieked in excitement.

"Who is that?" I asked in trepidation.

"Don't be afraid, Anna. I AM with you," The Figure

reassured me, comforting my hand in Its wounded hand.

"Excuse me! I've been wanting to talk to her the longest," the voice said as if it was maneuvering through a crowd while making its declaration. "Hello, Anna," the voice was trying to be polite, but it was clearly hostile, "I need your help!"

"I'm sorry," I interrupted, looking around and seeing no one there. "I cannot see you. Where are you coming from? Who are you?"

"Oh! Ladies, she still can't see us yet!" the voice said. I heard a cackle of noises after that: laughter, grumbling, screeches of panic, and commands.

"What is happening? Why can't I see them?" I asked The Figure, trying to be heard through the noises around us.

"Do you *want* to see them?" The Figure asked, causing me to reconsider that question.

"Is there a reason that I would not *want* to see them?" I asked.

"When you see them, your perception of everything else will change," The Figure replied. "I can help you see them. You just need to invite Me to show them to you."

I was about to question what The Figure said, but was interrupted by the voice again.

"I have become one of the strongest aspects about you lately, Anna. I am Loneliness. *Your* Loneliness." The voice kept talking. "You have been stuffing me with morsels ever since you let Guilt and Shame have precedence over you, and you have bound me to Grief over the past couple years. I am tired of eating and feeling the weight of Grief attached to me. I need you to help me get back into shape! I hate the way I look now, and…"

"Wait a second. I am not sure if I understand." The questions bounced around frivolously and made their way out of my head. "You are *my* Loneliness? *My* Loneliness? What does that even mean? How are you," I paused for the best word to use, "talking?"

The Figure turned to me and whispered, "This garden is called The Court Yard. This is the place where The Emotions live. Your judgements and choices inspire what grows here and what dies here. When you entered The Court Yard, you entered the center of *your* being. It has been chaotic here for a while, ever since you built the gate and created these impenetrable walls. There was a time when The Emotions walked with you freely around the forest, but they have been stuck in these walls since The Well crumbled. They come to that table when you make decisions." The Figure continued to explain while pointing to a table in the middle of The Court Yard, "As you make decisions, they feed off of them and grow stronger accordingly. You have fed some with your choices, and with those same choices, you have starved others. If you truly want to restore The Well and understand *The Door*, you will need to sit in here and talk to each one of them until you understand who they are and how to feed them so they can function properly."

"What had I gotten myself into? This is not what I had in mind for an adventure with The Figure. Adventures were supposed to be exciting and fun, and even though parts of The Court Yard were beautifully kept, I couldn't help but feel that this place was eerie and frightening. Talking to My Emotions sounded like something a crazy person does. What was the point of all of this?" I wearily pondered.

"Would you like to meet The Emotions, Anna?" The Figure asked, as if It heard my thoughts.

I didn't want to meet them. I just wanted to escape this adventure and go back to living in the forest the way I had done before The Well crumbled. However, it seemed like talking to them was the only way that I would be able to make progress toward repairing The Well though, so I acquiesced. With a deep sigh, I agreed to meeting The Emotions.

The moment I agreed, I heard the same bustle of commotion that I heard from afar prior to entering the gate. This time, I began to see the figures that belonged to those voices.

They were blurry to me at first. I could faintly see one of them smiling wearily at me as she led me to The Table.

When all of them stopped at The Table, I became excited. It looked like a party, with a bright white tablecloth covered with vases of flowers- I am assuming from this garden- and tiered platters filled with plain and berry scones, tea sandwiches, and other delightful treats.

The ghost-like Emotions sat in the chairs around The Table. All of them were in different colored dresses. After looking at their faces and seeing them more clearly, I realized they looked just like me! Each one had a slightly different disposition, but I felt as though I was looking at hologram-mirrors. I was baffled into silent disbelief.

"Let me talk to her," a sternly gruff voice said, interrupting my incredulity. The voice belonged to the woman wearing a violet dress. I could see her clearly. She stood up from her chair and walked to me. She had power in her stride, and I began to feel tense as she progressed in my direction. She was holding a trowel. "Well, well, well. If it isn't Little Miss Trying-To-Be-Perfect. You've made me quite strong with your attempts at making sure no one knows who you really are. You're welcome for my help."

"Wh-o, Wh-o are you?" I asked.

Once she stood in front of me, she leaned close to my face and, sensing my nervous disposition, she mocked, "Your worst nightmare," and unleashed a demonic cackle of ominous laughter. "Of course," she paused, crouched down until her mouth was right in front of my ear, and said "everyone here calls me Fear." I did not know if what she had just said was a joke or if she was serious. Either way, my body tensed up and became paralyzed for a moment. The only thing I could manage to move was my hand that was comforted inside of The Figure's.

Fear stepped aside and everyone else got up from The Table to introduce themselves. Loneliness, who was wearing a pink dress, was very pushy and louder than all the others. Grief was a silent little creature on her back. Hope, wearing orange, walked toward me with a kettle and hovered over me until I pulled out my cup and allowed her to pour some tea into it. Guilt and Shame walked together toward me in their long, flowing grey dresses. They finished each other's sentences as they tried to lure my cup away from me.

They all wanted a chance to speak. At the point when they were all trying to speak over each other, the noise got to be too much for me, and I plugged my ears and looked at The Figure.

"Everyone, go sit down at your seat, and let's talk to Anna one at a time," The Figure commanded. The Emotions obeyed.

Once seated, Fear looked at me, and I could feel my body tense again. My throat tightened, and my neck felt like warm needles pricking Inside. I became too warm to partake of the tea that Hope poured, so I pushed it as far away from me as possible, so as to not catch the evaporating steam on my face or hands.

"We wondered how long it was going to take you to arrive here, Anna. Some people never enter The Court Yard. We should feel lucky that you are one of the humans who has decided to come Inside and confront us- well, for lack of better terms- face-to-face," Loneliness informed with both excitement and trepidation while sitting next to Fear.

"Can someone please explain to me what is supposed to happen while I am here?" I asked, not knowing where to begin a conversation with those around me, my neck still feeling the sting of Fear's glare.

"As many protagonists whose stories you admire have come to this place in the forest, you have also followed in their footsteps. You were guided here by the fact that The Well is broken and you met The Figure. You now understand how to look at *The Door*, but you won't really understand all of it until you spend time here with us and then go out into the forest to see the validity of *The Door* for yourself. The commonalities will become increasingly clearer until everything you see will have a tightly-woven, serendipitous connection. Someday, you will write about all of this and share it with others, just as those writers you admire have done; only, *your* part of the story will be different from how they told *their* part of the same story."

I interrupted Loneliness, "Wait, there is only One story?" I thought about how The Figure separated *uni* and *verse* when It was trying to explain the same concept. "Is that why everything around us is called 'The Uni Verse'? Uni Verse: One Story. I get it!"

They all laughed, including The Figure.

"I will begin with this: although your story is your own, it is part of a larger One that includes others who have been here before you," said The Figure. "The Well has been part of *My* story from the beginning. You thought that it belonged to you, but you are mistaken. It belongs to Me, as does this forest and everything that lives here."

"I don't understand," I admitted, still curious.

"Of course you don't understand! If you did, you wouldn't be *here*. The first thing you need to learn is that your life's story is part of One larger story. You are the main character in *your* story, Anna, but your story is only *part* of His Story," chimed in Shame. She glanced at The Figure before continuing to talk to me. "You have been made to think that your story is the one that matters the most, and that is why you have never been able to share your own story coherently. You don't understand who you are or what your purpose is here."

I felt a sting in my chest. I knew this was true. Hope came to the rescue with tea. She pulled my cup closer to me and said, "The first lesson we can teach you is that, even though you are a very important part of the forest, everything you do with your time here is not about you."

"I don't understand," I sighed, confused that Hope was the one delivering this news. I took a sip. It was bittersweet tea. It would have been nice if someone handed me some cinnamon or maple syrup to add to it. Hope read my mind. She must have known how bittersweet her tea is.

"Like extracting sap from a tree," she glanced over at the maple trees with their leaves rustling in the wind, attached to the branches on the thick trunk that contained potential deliciousness inside, "this is going to take some time," assured Hope, "and we will all be here to help you. That is why you were brought to The Court Yard. You need to know how we can help you understand who *you* truly are," Hope paused for a brief second, smiled, and then continued, "while you are *here* in the forest."

"While I am *here*? Where else am I supposed to go? Am I not meant to stay in the forest?"

They all looked around at each other, attempting to delegate the task of answering that question with nods of permission to each other. Not one of them answered my question. Instead, Fear arose from her seat and, while walking to me, revealed, "Pushing that thought away is better for you right now, Anna. Here, give it to me." Fear grabbed me by the head harshly and shook me until the thought disappeared into what I assumed was her hands. She walked away with a clenched fist that she lowered to her side. As I watched her arm lower, I could see that her belly was distended. Maybe she had one too many of the delectable delights in front of us.

"We have some important things to talk about, Anna," The Figure directed us to progress our conversation toward the purpose of me being in The Court Yard.

We all talked for four hours. First, I learned about Loneliness and her struggle with Grief on her back and of her overindulgence in decision morsels to keep from becoming starved. The last time she was starved, Shame and Guilt took pleasure in tying her down to keep her from hurting herself again the way she does when she is hungry. Next, I learned about Shame and Guilt and their struggles to stay quiet when Loneliness disappears and Hope is content. They always seem to make sure that everyone else in The Court Yard remembers how horrible everyone *really* is, so that they can keep everyone in line. They are the rule-makers for etiquette at The Table in The Court Yard. It is the only way that they have been able to keep themselves alive. Then, I learned that Fear has been promiscuously seducing people in the forest. She controls most of what happens Outside of The Court Yard. She destroys what starts out as genuine relationships by using the trowel to put the stone wall up around The Court Yard and by planting cacti in the garden. She leaves occasionally to visit Anger and Ego at a place called The Swamp, and she always comes back stronger. Finally, I learned that Hope has been quietly observing all that happens in the garden. She gets her strength by understanding connections behind the symbolism of the forest and by trying to figure out how what is happening in The Court Yard will benefit everyone. She tries to keep everyone speaking softly as to not awaken Love, who sleeps in a red nightgown, snuggled up in an area close to the droopy delphinium and cacti. Hope often watches Love rest, and knows that one day, when Love awakens, The Court Yard will have loud, festive gatherings again.

While I learned all these things, I could see out of the corner of my eye that The Figure was smiling directly at me. Occasionally, I would glance over and our eyes would meet, and it was as if the more I learned in The Court Yard, the more I learned about The Figure, who was right about "intimacy." There was a natural intimacy that was beginning to grow through the insight I embraced.

"Let's just give it to her straight so that she doesn't miss the entire point of her being here like she has missed the point of being in the forest," Shame extended her arm out to hand me the napkin-lined basket filled with scones. Remembering Fear's pooch, I politely waved my hand in the air to decline.

"The Well is crumbled, and you are here to learn how to fix it because you are the one who destroyed it, Anna," Guilt, who was sitting right next to her best friend Shame, surprised me with her accusation.

"How did I destroy it? I wasn't even there!"

"*That* was how it was destroyed: neglect. You were supposed to watch over it and maintain it, but you were too busy running around in the forest and forgot to take care of it. So, the cracks in The Well became thicker and the water in The Well became stale and toxic," Shame continued what Guilt started.

"When you neglect The Well, it will poison you instead of nourish you. Then, you live your life in the forest running on toxic fumes. You become what you intake: poison. Your judgement is clouded by the poison, and you make poisonous decisions. Then, you act in ways that might poison others. You become an infection to those around you," Guilt chimed in, as Shame handed the basket of scones to Loneliness, who grabbed two and stuffed them into her mouth as quickly as possible.

"Haven't you seen what you have done to the trees around the forest?" Fear asked.

"What *I* have done?"

"Because *you* neglected The Well, the trees are being nourished with toxic water, too," Fear answered.

"Is that why they were trying to throw stones at me?" I asked The Figure.

"You will need to ask them yourself, Anna," The Figure answered.

"How do I do that?"

"First, we need to collect treasures from the forest to build a new well. We all need to go into The Mere Ore Forest together to gather some of the materials."

"I've never been to that part of the forest. Is it safe?"

"No, it is not safe at all. It is probably one of the most frightening places in the forest. The only place more frightening is The Swamp," said Fear with a slightly excited tone, as she ate a cookie from one of the platters on The Table.

"Are You coming with me?" I asked The Figure.

"You need to invite Me, remember?" The Figure smiled.

I couldn't help but smile back as I replied, "Will You please come with us into The Mere Ore Forest?" There was almost a slight flirtation in my voice, as if I was *actually* becoming more intimate with The Figure.

Hope ate a piece of chocolate and fluttered into excitement as she stood up and proclaimed, "Let's go! I know it will be scary, but we will all be there with you! Plus, I have heard that when you choose the right pieces of Ore from the forest, they turn into treasured gems or useful tools when you leave! We will need to collect as many of those as we can get to build the new well!"

She held one of my hands, and The Figure held the other. Together with Shame, Guilt, and Fear, I began the journey to The Mere Ore Forest. Loneliness and Grief stayed behind at The Court Yard.

The Mere Ore Forest

"You're sick! Just look at you!"

"Nothing you do is ever right!"

"If you could just look that way, you'd finally be happy!"

"Look at everyone else! They all have it together! What's the matter with you?"

"Nothing you have to say is valid! No one is going to listen anyway!"

The ghostly voices assaulted my ears. Along with the words, the invisible attackers propelled Ore in my direction. Each one hit me and burned like a fiery arrow.

The Emotions watched and waited for me to react.

"Why can't you just be more like...?"

"If people knew who you really are, they would run away."

"You are going to end up alone."

I heard more than enough. "Who are you?" I yelled out into the void of the voices.

"Come closer and see," said a vaguely familiar voice. I walked toward the sound of the voice as it beckoned me, "come closer, closer, closer. That is far enough. Now, what do you see?" the voice asked.

As I adjusted my eyes through the fog in the forest, I saw beams of light reflecting off the trunks of the trees. I wondered how the light reflected so brightly from the bark of each trunk. Walking toward one of the closest trees, I saw that the bark wasn't wood. It was glass.

When I looked through the glass, I could see that there was an old woman and a child inside of the trunk with their knees bent and folded, each cradling their own droopy, hanging head.

I placed my hand on the bark to see if my sense of touch matched my sense of sight. The bark was, in fact, a delicate, transparent glass. I jerked my hand away quickly when I realized that I startled the two inside of the trunk. Both of them lifted their heads, and my feet carried me backwards toward Fear. She caught me and held me tightly.

The old woman and child stood up and walked toward the exterior wall of their glass-bark prison. The child looked straight at me and mouthed my name.

I closed my eyes. I didn't want to be there anymore. Everything inside of me told me to run away, but Fear's grip on me held me in place. I was paralyzed.

"Anna," the old lady mouthed my name. The fingers on her left hand spread out and pressed against the glass. *What were they doing in the tree?* I wondered, as I closed my eyes.

"Anna," The Figure whispered my name. I couldn't hear the old lady or the child, but I could hear The Figure. "Open your eyes. Don't be afraid," The Figure's voice relaxed me enough to slide out of Fear's grip. Once free, I moved away from the glass tree, looking back at the two inside as they continued to mouth my name. Fear stood close by that tree. Shame and Guilt joined Fear.

With my head turned backwards toward the child's eyes, I didn't pay attention to see that there were more glass trees around me at that moment. I accidently bumped into the delicate trunk of a different tree and cracked it. There was a person inside of that one too. I ran to another tree, and there was another person! All of the people inside of the trees were crouched down in the fetal position. I could not see any of their faces.

Curiosity led me to one of the trees close by where I was standing. I recognized the clothes of the person inside. He wore a suit, and I could faintly smell the nostalgically nauseating scent of him from outside of the tree.

With Fear by my side, I walked up to the tree and knocked gently on the glass. He looked up at me.

I could feel my chest squeeze in pain as he looked me in the eye. I started to shake, and my throat started to close up as I tried to speak. "Can you hear me?" I paused as he rose, trying to brush the wrinkles in his suit. "What are you doing in there?" I asked him.

"Yes, I can hear you," his voice was clear, "and only *you* can tell me what I am doing in here, Anna."

I looked back at The Figure for answers, but the only response was the tears falling from Its encouraging eyes. As if the tears rippled down Its cheeks in visible-braille, I understood what they were communicating to me. The tears told me that I was the one that needed to find out the answers to my questions, and in doing so, I would experience pain.

"This is going to be difficult, isn't it?" I asked The Figure, who nodded as tears ran down Its cheeks. It remained silent as I began to listen to the voices from the tree again.

"You'll never measure up to my standards."
"If you don't change, you won't be loved."

The voices repeatedly echoed as I turned around and looked at the man. I remembered moments from our past, and then began my inquiry.

"You expected a lot from me, didn't you?" I asked the man.

"Of course, I did. It was my job."

"What was your job? To make me feel like I had to earn love?"

"Anna, it wasn't my intention for you to feel that you had to earn it."

"Then, why did I never feel good enough for your love?"

"If you understood my story, you would understand why I was the way I was."

"*Your* story? Why does it always have to be about you? Do you have any idea how I would struggle for days about making a decision that would be sure to please *you*? Do you know how many times I cried because I knew I could never live up to *your* standards? How about trying to understand *my* story before you ask me to do one more unselfish thing for *you*?" I didn't want to hear his story.

I felt a hand sting my shoulder from its touch. I turned around, thinking it was The Figure. "Anna, don't worry. I'm here," said a gruffly comforting voice.

"Who are you?"

"I am Anger. You called to me, so I came all the way from The Swamp to be here for you," Anger said, standing in front of me in a black dress with turquoise stripes, her sword drawn at the man in the glass-bark tree.

"I don't remember ever calling you." I mentioned to Anger.

"Anna, every time you put one of these people in the glass-bark trees, I helped you. You and I have been able to accomplish so much together. We even built the fence around The Court Yard together with Fear," Anger pronounced before revealing many other memories. She came closer to me for a friendly embrace. I started to shake again and pushed Anger away.

"This doesn't make sense. Why would *we* ever have a good relationship? The way I feel right now is not pleasant at all! How could I ever want to be around you?" I said, completely confused by what I was hearing.

"Anna, I embrace you when you are scared of..." Anger paused before finishing the sentence. She looked over at a woman standing by the glass tree next to Fear, Shame and Guilt. "Forgiveness," Anger said.

Anger put her arms around me, as I trembled more violently than before. She was right. I was frightened by the sight of Forgiveness, who walked toward me draped in a cobalt-blue dress with her long, grey hair pulled back tightly. She was carrying a bucket full of stones with her as she approached us. Anger quickly drew her sword and pointed it at Forgiveness, ready to attack her if she came any closer.

"Why am I scared of Forgiveness?" I whispered to Anger as she held me tightly with the arm not busy holding up the sword that was pointed in defense.

"You are scared of me because you understand how powerful I am," Forgiveness said slowly with strength behind each sound that emerged from her. She possessed a confidence and kindness that I coveted, but never experienced. "If you want my help, you need to let go of your unhealthy attachment to Anger."

"That's easy. I don't want Anger in my life," I said. However, immediately I felt uncertain.

"You don't mean that, Anna," Anger read my mind and then reminded me of how much she has done for me. "I protected you from him," she said as she pointed to the glass-bark tree with the familiar man inside. "You think I am the one who pursues you when it comes to him and everyone else trapped in the glass-bark trees, but you are the one who calls to me and runs into my arms. All these people can't hurt you as long as they are safely captured in the trees. If you set them free, who knows what they will do to you? We will continue to put people in here together. It is what we do. I am what comforts you anytime someone hurts you. All of these people hurt you, and when they did, I came to your rescue and put them in the glass-bark trees to keep you safe from them..."

"...and I am here to help you set them free," interrupted Forgiveness, "and that is what you are most afraid of..."

Forgiveness couldn't even finish her phrase before Fear came up from behind and put her hands over Forgiveness's mouth.

"I would be very careful what you say without Anna's permission," Fear growled in Forgiveness's ear and then turned to me, "Do you want me to take her away, Anna?"

I looked into Forgiveness's eyes and saw that Fear's grip on her did not affect her. Fear was the one affected by Forgiveness's calmness. I wanted Forgiveness's strength. I didn't want her to leave, but I was also afraid of what her power would do to me and the people in the glass-bark trees. *If what Anger said was true, and I freed these people. What would they do to me?*

Then, I remembered that Forgiveness had a bucket full of Ore.

"Forgiveness, what are these stones for?"

Forgiveness pointed to her covered mouth, and I told Fear to let go.

"Do you want to rebuild The Well *or* not?" Forgiveness asked.

"Of course, I do," I replied, thinking that it was an obvious answer. "Why would we use these stones to rebuild it?"

"That is not what we are using the stones for, Anna. They represent choices. You can use them to hurt these people *or* to set them free. You need to choose whether you will let Anger keep them here *or* let me help you free them."

Fear moved toward Forgiveness again, but Hope stepped in front of Fear and blocked her.

"Remember: *None* of us can do anything without your permission. What do you want, Anna?" Hope asked, not taking her eyes off Fear.

"Really?" I asked. "Fear seemed to silence Forgiveness without me asking her to…"

"Anna, you don't always need to verbally ask in order to give us permission," Fear corrected me.

"We are part of you, so your genuine desires give us permission," Hope explained. "In this circumstance, you just don't know what you want yet, so we don't know what to do until you make a decision."

"What do you want, Anna?" asked Forgiveness, even though she seemed to know the answer to the question.

"I don't know what I want," I admitted. "Can we all just talk for a minute without hurting each other?"

I was so involved with Fear, Forgiveness, and Hope, that I forgot that The Figure was with me.

"What do I do?" I turned back and asked The Figure.

The Figure looked at me deeply and whispered, "Go to The Tree."

There were trees all around me. I looked back at The Figure with confusion in my eyes, to which, The Figure nodded toward one of the trees. I turned around and saw the tree with the old lady and the child. I shook my head. I was too scared to go to that tree.

"Then, go to the others and come back to this one, Anna," Hope said to me, as if she knew my thoughts.

Just after Hope gave me permission to explore, I heard unpleasant, cackling laughter coming from one of the trees. I looked at Hope and Fear, who were standing right next to each other, back to back, and they both paradoxically nodded in approval of my progression toward the tree with the laughter.

When I was standing right in front of the cackle-filled, glass-bark tree, I could see a group of girls inside huddled together. When they saw me, they all turned to each other and let out a sound that made my heart squeeze into a painful ache. I knew these girls.

"There you are!" one of the girls said to me from inside the tree, as she stood up and walked to the edge of the glass-bark to face me. She had a necklace made of shells. It was beautiful! I found myself wanting a necklace too.

"What are you all doing in there together?" I asked.

"We have been waiting here until you let us out," said another one of the girls. She had a necklace with a tin heart pendant. I looked more closely at all the girls, and they all had a different necklace.

"Why do I need to let you out?"

"Because it is the only way for you to free yourself from us," said the girl with the shell necklace.

"It is the only way for you to find your necklace," the girl with the tin-heart necklace added.

"You mean, I get a necklace if I let you out?"

"Yes. Well, if you let everyone out."

"Everyone?"

"Look around, Anna," the girl with the tin necklace continued and pointed to the glass-bark trees around me.

"How do I let *all* of you out?" I inquired. Then, I saw the girl with the shell necklace point to Forgiveness, who had the bucket of stones in her hand.

"Forgiveness?" I whispered.

"Yes," Forgiveness answered back.

Fear and Anger started walking toward me. Forgiveness kept her eye on me, as if she was waiting for permission to come to me.

I looked back at the girls. Fear and Anger came toward me more quickly. Hope began to back away. I could hear the girls begin to laugh again from inside the glass bark.

The laughter brought Fear and Anger by my side. I faced the girls.

"I know you," I told them. "You: the one with the shell necklace," I looked at her, and Anger held my hand. "You were the one who first broke my trust in friendship. You used to make fun of me as a way to become popular." I could feel Anger pull me into a hug. "Because of you, I was unable to feel safe being vulnerable with females. Because of you, I felt like I was a disappointment as a friend. Because of you, I rejected opportunities to get close to women. Because of you, I felt like I would always be in competition with girls, so I just stayed away from them." I turned to the girl with the tin necklace. "And you! You accepted me as a friend, as long as I did everything you

51

wanted me to do. As long as I was following your agenda, you were nice to me, but when I decided that what you were doing was wrong, and I refused to play your petty games of gossip and competition, you made it so uncomfortable to be at school that I decided to ditch class or pretend to be sick, just so that I was not around you!" I verbally unleashed every hurt and pain that each of the girls caused me, all the while, Fear was cheering me on and encouraging me. Anger comforted me by holding me tighter.

The more I confronted them, the louder the girls laughed, and the tighter Anger confined me. I wanted to break free; I wanted the laughing to stop, but I didn't know how to make that happen. I turned my head away from that tree and saw The Figure. I could see the wounds on Its folded hands.

I looked at Forgiveness, with her bucket of stones. Readiness to silence the laughter pulled me toward her. Anger became weaker as my focus remained on Forgiveness and The Figure, who both nodded at me and smiled. I felt a strength surge through me.

"No!" I said as powerfully calm as humanly possible, freeing my arms from Anger's embrace and motioning that I did not want Fear and Anger to say or do any more. The Word gave me the strength I needed over them. No longer having their precious power, Fear and Anger sat quietly on the ground. I turned to Forgiveness and motioned for her to join me.

"What do I now?" I asked Forgiveness.

"I need to introduce you to a friend of mine," she answered. She directed my attention to the pools of water on the ground around me. I remembered how thirsty I was. When I knelt near one of the puddles, I could see words floating inside over my distorted reflection. I took my cup and dipped it inside of the puddle. The words faded away, along with my reflection.

"Don't drink from these puddles, Anna," a loud voice warned me. "Come over here to quench your thirst." I stood up and walked toward the voice. I looked at Forgiveness, who nodded in approval toward the voice.

Then, she walked with me down to the edge of the river that flowed through the forest. I saw a woman with long, flowing grey hair that was sprinkled with flowers. On the top of her head was a crown that contained the most beautiful jewels I had ever seen! Her neck was adorned with iridescent pearls. She smiled at me. "Hello, Anna. I have been waiting a long time for this moment." I was awestruck by how soothing and powerful her voice sounded and how beautiful all her features shone from her face. Her eyes sparkled like the jewels on her crown and pierced through me like diamonds on glass.

"Give me your cup, so I can fill it here for you," the woman commanded.

"Who are you?" I could barely get out my question.

"Surely, you can figure out who I am, Anna."

"How would I know you?"

"Didn't you see images of me while looking at *The Door*?"

I tried to recollect seeing a woman on *The Door* that matched the description of the woman standing in front of me. It was as if she could read my mind. She mouthed the word "twenty," and I knew she was talking about the 20th panel of *The Door*.

"Etymologically, the title of the twentieth panel meant 'bring forth The Word into action.' You are here to learn how to put what you learned from *The Door* into action."

I handed her my cup, and she dipped it into the flowing river next to her feet. I took a sip, and my eyes grew wide with satisfaction and wonder. After even just that one sip, my whole being felt rejuvenated. I wanted to continue my conversation with the woman.

"The Figure tried to guide me through understanding *The Door*," I was saying as I saw The Figure startle me in Its approach. "Oh! You frightened me a bit," I said to The Figure, who was walking with Fear toward me. Anger was not with them, and Fear's disposition was softened.

"Then, I see you have met Wisdom," The Figure chuckled, as I stood a bit perplexed at this new understanding.

"Wisdom? I thought you would be more difficult to find than this!" I said. The truth was, it had not been easy. It just felt that way now that I was actually there.

"Here, let me show you what I have been waiting to share with you for so long," Wisdom reached out her hand and invited me to walk with her along the edge of the river. I took Wisdom's hand in mine. The Figure and Fear were with us on our journey alongside the river and participated in our conversation.

I learned that The Mere Ore Forest is a place for contemplation and reflection. It is where I make choices that will either help or hurt me. This was also where I would eventually find Freedom. According to Wisdom, I needed to meet them here to prepare me for what awaited me at The Swamp. Since I had already been introduced to Wisdom, it was time for me to let her help guide me to find Freedom.

"In order to find Freedom, you have some work to do, Anna. It will not be easy. You need all of us to help you, and we will be here for you, but it is you who needs to persevere through destroying what has made you sick," Wisdom assured.

"What made me sick was being thirsty and not being able to

quench my thirst. The Well has already shattered. What else needs to be destroyed?" I asked, taking the last sip of river water that was in my cup. I looked into the now empty cup and wondered when I would be able to drink again.

Wisdom averted her eyes from mine and looked at the glass-bark trees around us. I looked at them too.

"Is Freedom inside of one of these trees?" I asked.

"Freedom is inside of all of them, Anna," Wisdom answered my daunting question. Then, she asked an even more daunting question. "Are you ready to find her?"

I took a deep breath, and something Inside began to feel warm, as if a match was ignited and sparked light and heat within me. I nodded in response to Wisdom's question.

"So, where would you like to begin?" Wisdom asked.

I looked at the tree that contained the girls with the necklaces. Something inside told me to wait and go back to that tree later. My eyes scanned the forest and came across a grouping of trees that huddled close together, as if they were sharing the same root system. I walked to the grouping of glass-bark trees until I could see who was inside of them.

My chest clenched when I saw the faces of those inside of that grouping of trees. Part of me wanted to run away. I didn't want to be in The Mere Ore Forest anymore.

"You have a choice, Anna," Hope encouraged. "You can stay here and free these people, *or* you can leave them all inside of the glass-bark trees. The choice is yours. You will not be able to rebuild The Well if you don't free them."

"What are you going to do?" Fear asked. "Either choice will affect your life. If you leave them here, you are safe from them. They can't hurt you again."

"...but if you leave them here, their voices will always haunt you," Hope interrupted. "Could you imagine what it would be like to not hear their voices echoing in the forest anymore?"

I thought about what both Fear and Hope said. Forgiveness and Anger stood side-by-side, playing an invisible game of tug-of-war, using my decision as the rope.

"Can I just let a few of them out?" I asked.

"You can, but you won't find Freedom until you let all of them out," Forgiveness warned.

"Anna, you have made it here. Most people never come to their Mere Ore forest. You should be proud of yourself. You have us all here to help you, too," Hope took my hand and gave me a reassuring squeeze.

My thoughts whipped into a whirlwind of "ifs and shoulds" between "this *or* that."

I surveyed the trees to see where I wanted to begin. Anger stood next to the tree with the girls; Shame was next to the grouping of trees that contained men from failed relationships. Guilt was near the man with the suit. I looked around at all the trees. I walked up to some and peered deeply inside, making eye-contact with each person who was trapped. I talked to some of them, but I did not stay long enough to free any of them.

Whenever I was reluctant to do something in the past, I was advised to "get the hardest part done first." Forgiveness stood next to the tree that contained an old woman and a child. The child was familiar, but I had never met the old woman. On my way toward them, my legs became weak. I tripped over one of the roots protruding from the ground. I fell and was wounded. My knees and hands colored the ground with sprinkles of blood. The child and the old woman fell when I fell. It was then that I knew who both of them were. It terrified me. I didn't want to move closer. I didn't want to talk to them. I felt I let the child down; I felt too weak to free them. I was at a loss. I didn't want to move forward, and I didn't want to move backwards. I wondered why I ever came to The Mere Ore Forest in the first place. I wondered how I would get out.

I laid on forest floor and wept. Anger came to my side and held me as I shivered. I let her hold me this time. I wanted to scream. I was hurt, and I didn't want to be in that forest anymore. I didn't want to confront any of the people in the trees; especially the old woman and the child. I didn't want to do what it took to free them. I also didn't want to live with those haunting voices anymore. I had to make the decision quickly because Fear started to move closer to me. She was ready to carry me out of the forest. If I let Anger and her comfort me out of this situation, they would regain their old power, and I would never find Freedom. I was very good at running away from situations like this, but that choice is what brought me to this moment. Something needed to change.

I looked to The Figure for reassurance. We gazed at each other in silence. My toes started to feel stronger, and I became more grounded. The strength moved up my legs into my torso and arms. Finally, my whole being had a strength that I never felt before. The Figure nodded at me in approval and smiled, knowing that I had made my decision. I stood up, pushed Anger away, held up my hand to stop Fear, and yelled, "No more!"

Fear jumped back, and Hope turned to me. "Hope, I need you," I begged.

"Why would you want the 'delusional one' to join you, Anna?" asked Anger. "I am a much more reliable source in this situation. You are safer keeping these people where they belong. If you let them out, Hope will just mess with your mind like she did before with all of them."

"I want Hope," I said, determined to find Freedom.

Fear and Anger backed away, and Hope walked with me to the tree with the old woman and the child.

"Anna, I'm so sorry for what I did to you! When you were this young, you had no idea what was ahead of you. I made choices that hurt you, and I can't go back and redo them. You are so precious, and I should have paid more attention to your strengths and needs and dreams. Please forgive me!"

"You are incapable of forgiving! You are not my friend! You are my enemy! Why did I think that I could trust you? I am such an idiot! Look at you! You are sick!" the child screamed loudly, echoing the words of the ghostly voices.

"I will make things better now. We will still have troubles, but I am stronger now."

The old woman looked at me and Hope, standing next to each other. She smiled. Fear and Anger continued to stay away, breathing heavily as they watched my interaction with the old woman and the child.

"I will get you out of there!" I yelled and hit the tree with my fist, making a knocking sound. It hurt, but I continued to hit it again and again. I opened my clenched fist and started to hit the tree even harder. Since my hands were becoming weaker each time they encountered the glass-bark, I picked up the stone from Forgiveness' bucket and started to hit the glass-bark. On the last strike, I felt a sting in my finger from a crack in the glass. As I pulled away, shards of glass went into my finger and the trunk shattered. All the glass-bark trunks shattered at the same time and all the people inside were freed. Shame and Guilt ran after them out of The Mere Ore Forest.

As I looked up to defend myself against all the people who were no longer trapped in the glass-bark trees of The Mere Ore Forest, I was baffled to see that no one was there.

Looking at the shattered glass on the trunk of the tree, I saw my fractured reflection piercing back at me. The one I had been screaming at the entire time was me. The ghostly voices I heard upon entering The Mere Ore Forest were my own.

That was why the child repeated them. That child was my younger self and the old woman was my future self. The trees were not glass, as I had originally thought. I realized why *all* the trees shattered when I used Forgiveness's stone to free the old woman and the child. The glass-bark was comprised of mirrors, and my perception of who was trapped inside was deceived by my own assumptions of who I was and how others interacted with me.

I needed to understand how to forgive myself first. Putting these people in the trees was not to protect myself against them; it was to protect them against me: not having boundaries, saying yes when I meant no, giving while expecting reciprocation. I realized that I was to blame for the resentments I held. None of these people could have hurt me without my permission. These people were trapped in the trees because I imprisoned them with my own actions and beliefs.

I hurt myself, and it was my own fault. I blamed all the people in the trees in The Mere Ore Forest for so long that I didn't realize that the entire time, I was only upset at others because of what I saw in myself. The faces of the others were just a mirage for what I didn't want to see this whole time; I was my own nemesis.

I knelt on the ground and wept the deepest that I have ever wept. My hands melted into the softened ground; blood from my wounds mixed in with debris and mud. Forgiveness knelt next to me and held me.

My body trembled as water leaking from my eyes carried years of hurt from deep within. The water from my tears must have nourished the roots of the glass-bark trees, and they regrew instantly into new mirror trees. When I stood up and investigated the glass-bark trees, I saw that my reflection was no longer fractured. I finally saw who I really was, and she was a beautiful mess.

"Hello, Anna," a voice greeted me.

I looked up and knew who it was right away. I crawled over to her feet and kissed them.

"Get up and give me a hug when you are ready," she demanded with a chuckle in her tone. I stood up, a completely dirty mess, and embraced her. As she held me, I felt like a child. I had known her once when I was a child, but she was trapped in The Mere Ore Forest for many years, waiting there for me by all the old glass-barked trees.

"Freedom?" I asked, not wanting to assume it was her.

"Yes, Anna," she confirmed. "It is so nice to see and be seen by you again." Our reunion was celebrated by Hope and Wisdom clapping in excitement.

"Here," Wisdom put something over my head that draped around my neck. "The only way you could have been safe wearing this is if you found Freedom. This belongs to you and only you. This is a precious gift from The Figure. Keep it safe."

I looked down and saw a necklace. I had my own, just like

the girls in the tree! Each of their necklaces were specific to who they are. I remember seeing parts of their personality symbolically embedded into the details of their necklace. I looked at the details of my necklace and saw that it had pearls, sapphires, and graphite. I also saw a key made from one of Forgiveness's stones and pieces of shattered mirror that looked like rugged diamonds. There were other elements that I could not identify at the time, but all of them carefully placed together made quite a treasure. I also noticed places where pieces were missing.

"You will find the treasures that go in those places," Hope reassured me. She smiled as she admired the necklace on me.

"It's time to prepare The Table at the Court Yard," The Figure addressed The Emotions, and they all nodded in agreement. Even Fear nodded. Her disposition was that of a supportive friend. "Hope, I want you to take Anna for a walk to The Secret Cave. You two have much to discuss on the way there," The Figure turned to me and smiled, "I will meet you at *The Door* when you are ready. Don't forget that, even though I will be waiting at *The Door*, I AM still with you, always." The Figure eyed the necklace and then brought the attention back to my eyes.

"I can't wait to see You at *The Door* again!" I said as I hugged The Figure tightly. I was beginning to grow attached to The Figure.

"It's time for us to go. You have so many more treasures to find, Anna," Hope giggled as she invited my hand into hers. I took Hope's hand into mine, and we began walking on a path together through a part of the forest where the sun shone through blossom-filled mirror trees on the way to The Secret Cave.

Swamped

On our way to The Secret Cave, we noticed a sign on the side of the path. It was an invitation to what looked like a festive gathering. Hope urged me to stay on the path, but I felt empowered by my experience in the Mere Ore forest. I had an inner pull to accept the invitation and veer off the path for just a little while. After all, I had just met Freedom and felt entitled to make that decision, so I accepted the sign's invitation.

I followed signs that led me to a place filled with very entertaining activities! Hope said she would not go with me any further and would see me when I was ready to come back to the path that leads to The Secret Cave. As much as I wanted Hope with me, I was heavily drawn into the excitement that awaited me off the path. I was stronger and more independent now. Hope would just need to wait.

It didn't take me long before I reached what could only be described as complete pandemonium. My eyes darted in all directions, playing ping-pong with the variety of sights in front of me. Amidst the chaos, I narrowed my focus to an area with an outdoor couch that had a television approximately 12 feet in front of it. A creature was sitting on the couch vigorously dunking a remote controller into a glass of turbid water and cursing at the television for not working. It only had one narrowly opened eye in the center the mass that I assumed to be its head. From the neck down, the rest of the creature looked like a child.

"What is that creature doing?" I whispered to myself.

"Oh! That is the creature that Freedom and I created. Its

name is Carelessness," said a voice that I thought I had heard before but did not quite recognize at that moment. I looked around, remembering that the others were not with me. I was alone with someone who I hadn't formally met yet.

"Who are you?" I asked the gloriously put-together woman in front of me.

"Oh! Dear, sweet Anna; I am the one who helps you "win" others over. I am the one who keeps you from looking like a fool. I make you everything you want to be," she said in the most eloquently articulate voice I ever heard. "I," she paused and placed her hand over her chest as the vowel response lingered in the air, "am Pride," she calmly informed me. She politely and delicately extended her hand out for me to shake. My hand magnetized to hers, and I felt confidence surge through my body as our hands linked.

Like the other Emotions, she looked like me, but she was a much more refined and sophisticated version of me than I had ever seen in the mirror. Her hand, although initially appearing dainty, was strong and welcoming. I didn't want to let go. I wanted the power she had in her grip.

She continued her explanation as she let go of my hand and pointed to the creature on the couch. "Carelessness has the tendency to do whatever it thinks is best without really knowing the nature of things. It doesn't know that all it needs to do is lift the remote and click the Power button to turn on the television. Poor little thing. Since it is free to explore its own way of viewing the world, it refuses to read instructions, so it spends most of its existence frustrated. Although a bit dim, it is quite amusing, isn't it?" Pride let out a chuckle of approval, encouraging Carelessness to continue exercising its liberty to treat the remote however it wanted to, even if it was contrary to its purpose. "That's right, my dear, keep exploring. You might get it to work one of these days." Pride looked at me and rolled her eyes.

Thinking I could talk some sense into Carelessness, I walked over and sat down next to it on the couch. "Don't you know that the remote doesn't belong in water? If you keep dunking it in there, you will ruin it, silly!"

"Don't tell me what to do! I can do what I want with what I want when I want and how I want," it said in a childish squeak, splashing dingy water on itself as it forcefully shoved the remote into the glass while keeping eye contact with me.

Seeing the water splashing around reminded me of my initial thirst at the beginning of this journey. After meeting Wisdom, I hadn't felt thirsty. Now that I was sitting next to Carelessness, my throat felt dry and dirty, as if I was breathing in dust.

I took my eyes off Carelessness and soaked in the scenery around me. Everything was perfectly chaotic and busy. There were other creatures that looked like Carelessness splashing in the pools of water surrounding the area by the couch. It was then that I realized the scorching heat that began to penetrate my skin. I wanted to jump in the pool with the creatures. Carelessness must have noticed my desires, because it grabbed my hand, pulled me off the couch, and led me to the busiest pool.

Even though it was murky, the water looked so inviting! I was about to jump in when I was suddenly paralyzed with hesitation. I saw my blurred, rippled reflection, distorted with the waves that the creatures were making as they splashed. I remembered my reflection in the Mere Ore Forest.

"Go on into the water, dear," a voice reassured me. "You *deserve* it."

I looked up at the one who just spoke to me and saw the most breathtaking women I had ever seen. Every inch of her was perfection.

"Oh my!" The beautiful woman looked at me and smiled. *She* was admiring something about *me*. I liked the way that felt. "What do you have there?" she asked, reaching for my necklace. I remembered what Freedom said about being careful choosing with whom I showed the necklace to, so I politely tucked my necklace back under the cover of my dress. The woman let out a laugh and snorted.

"I do that too," I giggled, with a snort.

"We are very similar, Anna," she leaned in and put her hand on my shoulder, attempting to earn my trust through her words and mannerisms. I was still reluctant to let her close to me, even though she was beautiful and smelled lovely, which was a nice change from the pungent surroundings of the swampy area around me.

"Why is someone like *you* here?" I asked.

"This is my home," she answered. "I oversee everything that happens here. I guess you can say that I am the Queen of The Swamp."

"Is that why you look and smell nicer than anything else here?"

"Of course! That is my job! That is my purpose! If I don't look this way, none of the Idles will be inspired by me."

"The Idles?"

"All of the creatures, like Carelessness, here in The Swamp are Idles. They come here to relax and get nourished. I treat them well and inspire them with my beauty. Sometimes, all they need to survive is just to bask in my beauty. Beauty does that, Anna. It inspires *more* beauty. Just look at the Taj Mahal. Beauty in a person inspired beauty in a building. Beauty inspires songs and poetry. The beautiful things in this forest are all inspired by…"

"Beauty," I finished her sentence. We both giggled and snorted. "Isn't beauty subjective, though?" I asked.

"Yes. That is what makes it wonderfully mysterious and sometimes unattainable," The Queen of The Swamp said as she giggled, snorted, and clapped her hands together in delight.

I thought about and realized that what she said is mostly true in my life.

I felt an instant connection to The Queen and wanted to learn more about her. "How long have you been The Queen here?"

"Off and on for about 39 years. If I do my job correctly, it is simple, but there are enemies in the forest that want to see this place --and me-- destroyed."

"Destroyed? Why?"

"I have an enemy in this forest, and It wants me to be under Its submission."

"Who is your enemy?"

"What? You can't *figure* It out on your own?" she asked looking down at me with her bright, piercing eyes.

We were interrupted by two women progressing quickly in our direction. When they finally arrived, I recognized one of them right away.

"Anna, wwwe… heard yooour… scream… from… The Court Yard! We're…here!" Fear unnecessarily reassured me, gasping for air in between syllables.

"Who is that with you?" I asked, pointing to the disheveled, timid woman holding hands with Fear.

"Would ...you like to... introduce yourself?" Fear said to the woman, who was now hiding behind Fear, shaking its head. Fear rolled her eyes, "Anna, this...is Insecurity." Fear caught her breath before continuing. "We both ran as fast as we could after we heard you scream out for us."

"I never screamed," I corrected Fear's assumption.

"We heard you loud and clear," Fear contradicted. "Now that we are here, how can we be of assistance?"

"Well, well, well, look who has gone soft with servitude," the Queen of The Swamp said to Fear. "I hardly recognized you, serving Anna when she used to serve you. How does it feel to be so low on the totem pole?" The Queen laughed and snorted. "We've missed you here in The Swamp, but we haven't missed that little...thing... you brought with you. She defeats all that we stand for here in The Swamp."

Insecurity tried to run away, but her feet sunk into the thick mud of The Swamp around her, almost grabbing at her feet to paralyze her.

"Anna, would you like for me to get rid of this...thing... for you?" asked The Queen of The Swamp.

"How would you do that?" I asked.

"Well," she paused and glanced at the ground while pondering, "we would give you a makeover, and she," pointing at Insecurity, "would disappear for a while."

"A makeover? What do you mean?"

"Well, let's see," The Queen pondered for a moment as she examined me from head to toe. What if we changed your hair color so that people who see you know that you have made some changes to yourself from that old, drab person that you didn't like seeing in your reflection of the waters in The Swamp a few minutes ago. We can change you to look like the fabulously glamorous person you want everyone to think you are now that you found Freedom." After she looked at my hair and studied my face for a while, she finally blurted out in excitement, "I know! Let's cut your hair and change it from brunette to blonde! That'll show everyone that the old you is gone, and the new you is ready for an adventure!"

I became excited at the opportunity to make some changes. Even though I thought I accepted the beautiful mess that I am, I really didn't like who I saw in the reflection of The Mere Ore Forest trees or the waters in The Swamp. I thought that the people who rejected me before would be more likely to want me around after I changed.

"Ok! Let's do it!" I said with both anticipation and excitement.

The Queen snapped her fingers, and little Idles came running to her. Carelessness was among them, holding the drenched remote. "It's time for a change. Do whatever it takes to make sure Anna looks and feels like a new woman!"

The creatures scurried about making sure that they changed anything that they possibly could change about me. My long, brown hair was cut off and dyed blonde, and my somewhat conservative clothes became more revealing. One of the Idles brought me books that taught me how to change my perspective of myself and others. Another Idle put a device in my hand that allowed me to share all the changes with other people, so that maybe they would contact me and want to spend time with me now that I changed.

"Something is not quite right yet," The Queen told the Idles. "I love the color of her hair, but she looks so much better with long hair."

One of the Idles brought long strands of blonde hair to The Queen. She attached the pieces to my head. As each one went in, The Queen ran her fingers down the length of the hair, tousling it in delight.

After the transformation took place, I was brought before a mirror and saw someone who I did not recognize. I knew that was the whole point, but that moment, like Hope's tea, had more bitter than sweet attached to it. "Look at you, Anna! So pretty! I just love this new you!" The Queen looked at me in proud approval, but she had a slight disdain in her disposition. Maybe she was a bit jealous. She still had her long, brown hair.

"I love *your* hair and think *you* are beautiful," I said while attempting to run my fingers through the Queen's long hair the way she did with mine.

When my hand got close to touching her, she quickly pulled away and then ran across the waters of The Swamp to the other side.

"Where are you going?" I called after her, trying to follow her across The Swamp. The water was knee-deep, and my feet started to get stuck in The Swamp as I chased after her. I wondered how she was able to walk across without falling into the murky waters.

"She runs away every time you are close to taking off her mask, Anna," said Pride, who reappeared and walked closer to me with Fear. I couldn't see Insecurity, but I knew she was still hiding behind Fear.

"I didn't know she was wearing a mask. Is that why she looks flawless?" I asked Pride.

"Of course! But it is your perception of flawless that created that mask. If Acceptance ever came to The Swamp, she would defeat The Queen. Once defeated, The Queen will look like you," Pride paused for a moment, "well, the you that you were before the new you. Even though you are not even close to perfect now, *you* are the reason she is hiding. You *want* her to hide."

"Why would I *want* her to hide?"

"Anna, she means well, but The Queen and the Idles contributed to the crumbling of The Well. You cannot rebuild it without finding Acceptance. The Queen knows that, so she does whatever she can to keep Acceptance away. When Acceptance is around, her mask falls off. Acceptance needs your help to win her battle with The Queen," Fear enlightened me.

"I didn't know I had that power over 'The Queen of The Swamp.'" I said mimicking imaginary quotations in the air. I laughed with Fear.

Pride took our laughter as a personal insult, and salvaging every ounce of herself that remained, walked away from us.

"You can have that power, but for now, Shame and Guilt still have a hold on you. If you really want to find Acceptance so that she can help you reveal and defeat The Queen, you need to go to The Secret Cave and set the prisoners free, which will take control away from Shame and Guilt. Then, you need to come back to The Swamp with Acceptance and find The Queen." Fear knew so much about this place.

"That does not sound like a very pleasant task."

"Which is less pleasant: confronting Shame and Guilt or not finding Acceptance? As soon as you can put Shame and Guilt in their place, The Queen and Acceptance can have a fair battle and you will finally have what you need to rebuild The Well. Until then, you will be running around the forest at the mercy of

Shame, Guilt, Carelessness, and The Queen."

"When you put it that way, it is hard not to see the logic behind the 'right' choice."

I looked around The Swamp. I knew that I could not cross to the other side without guidance. I had never been to The Secret Cave and did not know what I would find there. Something inside me started to tremble.

"I'm here, Anna," said Fear. "What do you need?"

"Can you please be a guide for me as we go to The Secret Cave? I don't know what to expect. Just make sure not to hold on too tight and paralyze me this time."

"You and I have a different understanding of each other after The Mere Ore Forest, Anna," Fear said as she rubbed her stomach below her belly button. I was confused by her gesture, but ignored it as she continued to speak, "You lead the way. I'm here for you." Fear, with Insecurity invisibly following behind, extended her hand in an invitation to walk together.

We met Hope where I left her. She took me by the other hand, and we all headed to The Secret Cave.

Hope, Fear, Insecurity, and I saw The Figure at *The Door* on our way to The Secret Cave. I felt like The Figure disapproved of my new look, even though It opened Its arms and welcomed me back to *The Door*. I ran into The Figure's open arms and began to weep. My tears felt dry, even though they sprung out of my eyes like the splashing water of the murky pools at The Swamp.

"I didn't think You would recognize me. Look at what The Queen of The Swamp did! I didn't like who I was then, but now that I am here with You again, I realize that what I have become now is even worse! Nothing about these changes represents who

I am. I know that was the point, but I just want to be my real self and to like who I really am," I could barely get the words out in between my sobs.

"Some of the things that you take refuge in are the things that cause you the very grief you are trying to avoid, and some of the things you try to avoid are the very things that will give you actual peace," The Figure said, tossing around my fake, blonde hair in Its hands.

Feeling embarrassed, I pulled away from our embrace and looked away. I was ready to find myself; my true, authentic self. I wanted the peace that came from being ok with who I really am, but I didn't know how I could obtain it.

"Anna, I think it is time for you to confront Shame and Guilt in The Secret Cave," said a voice I had not heard before. "Your journey isn't over yet. You still have a long way to go before we retrieve all of the materials to fix The Well."

"Who are you?" I asked the voice.

"You came back to look for me. You will usually find me here with The Figure. I am Acceptance, and I have been waiting so long for you to want to find me. If you invite me on the rest of your journey, I will help you find the rest of the materials to rebuild The Well." I know I should have been happy to find her, but she was only a faint, ghostly mirage and she scared me.

"What more do I need to do in order to fix The Well?" I was tired and wanted to know the quickest way to rebuild The Well. "I thought that this journey would lead to a better life: an easier life. All I have experienced so far has caused more hurt. When is this supposed to get better?" I started to cry again. "Every time I encounter something new in this forest since The Well crumbled, I feel more and more like I have been living a lie; as if everything that I knew before was just one large deception! Please tell me when this is supposed to get better!" I begged for answers. Ironically, the more I ranted how I truly felt, the more visible, and less scary, Acceptance became.

The Emotions were quiet for a while. Then, The Figure began to speak. "Anna, we share the same desire and the same struggle. There is an antagonist to My story. It is your antagonist, too. The Antagonist is deceptive about everything, especially about who I AM. When Shame, Fear, and Ego are trained to become stronger than Hope, Acceptance, and Love, The Antagonist has more control, and I am left to wonder and wait until the people in the forest recognize Me for who I AM."

"I'm glad I can recognize You," I tried to assure The Figure.

"Anna, you still don't know some of the most important aspects of who I AM. If you seek to understand, I will gladly reveal whatever you want to know. Like you, I want to be known for who I really AM."

"I don't know where to begin," I confessed.

The Figure turned to look at *The Door*. I remembered that *The Door* contained The Figure's story. I looked at the panels. There were so many intricate details of The Figure's story carved and brought to life in each of the panels. It was overwhelming to attempt to understand everything involved.

"Who are You? I want The Truth," I finally asked.

"I AM all you want, Anna."

"What does that mean?"

"Look with your eyes and hear with your ears, and you will know." The Figure directed my eyes to *The Door*.

We talked for many months while looking at the panels. The more time I spent with The Figure at *The Door*, the clearer the details of the panel became. After much of *The Door* was clearer to me, I asked, "So, all of those panels make up One story? It is almost as if Your story was a quilt of stories over the course of history. Some of those panels explain parts of the story that have not even happened yet."

"Very few people see the panels as One story woven together, and even fewer understand that it is My story. As I told you before, The Antagonist crouches here at *The Door* often and preys on those who have the desire to deepen their understanding of the panels."

"Where is The Antagonist now?"

"When I AM here, The Antagonist hides."

"Why?"

The Figure was quiet for a moment, and then changed the subject, "How did you like the ending of My story?"

"What I liked most is that You won The Battle."

"Yes, I did." The Figure smiled at me and then became very serious. "Anna, because I won the battle, the story in this forest is already finished. Even *this* part of the story, the one we are living right now, has been written. It is difficult for you to understand because you have only known life here in the forest. That is why I carved *The Door* and put it here in the forest. I *want* you to think deeply and understand. I *want* you to seek the places beyond this forest; those places already know the end of My story. Here in the forest, among the trees in the woods, we are just acting out what has already been written. Haven't you heard the phrase, 'Life is a stage…'?"

"Of course! I taught Shakespeare's work to my students. I have to say that even his language is easier to understand than the panels on *The Door.* I really enjoy both of your languages, though.

They are so complex that it forces the audience to think for themselves or be eternally confused. The difference is that I don't have Shakespeare here to ask questions about his intentions. I have You here to explain *The Door*. What do You think Shakespeare meant when he wrote 'Life is a stage…?'"

"Who do you think gave Shakespeare the idea?" The Figure chuckled in Its own humor and then gave an explanation. "This life is just one *stage* of your soul's experience. What Shakespeare meant had double meaning. As you know, he liked to *play* with language." We both giggled and The Figure continued, "This life *is* a *stage*; it is not the entire play. It is the platform for which we allow the story to play out. It is also just one *stage*. It is just one phase of the Uni-Versal experience. There is a backstage; there is an audience; there is a director; there is a script-writer."

"There is even a stage door," I chimed in, pointing to *The Door* in front of us while trying to participate in the cleverness, as I understood the way The Figure was playing with language to explain something so complex to me. Even with the analogy and added humor, the concepts were still difficult for me to grasp. "I am not sure I understand all of what You are saying, but what I do know is that Your story is beautifully woven together. I would love to see it as a stage play!"

"Anna, it is, and you are part of it. You are living it right now. *That* is what Shakespeare was trying to tell you."

"I'm so confused."

"Do you remember this panel?" The Figure pointed to the 19th panel in the 139th section. "You mentioned a quilt earlier. You are part of My story; My quilt. I AM the one who stitched you into the quilt. I AM the author of My story. I AM part of the One who loves you so much that I wrote myself into the play here," The Figure pointed to the 40th- 43rd panels, "so that I could tell people of the forest who I AM and to show the extent I AM willing to go for them to experience and know Love."

I thought about Love and wondered if she was still sleeping in The Court Yard. I really wanted to talk to her. I'm sure she and I had conversations before, but I really didn't *know* her. I looked up at the panels and saw that The Figure was rejected, wounded, and killed so that It could introduce me to Love in her most authentic and awakened self.

"Is that how You got these wounds?" I asked, holding onto The Figure's hands and examining them. "These wounds were for Love! You told me that when I first saw Your hands, but I didn't understand at the time. I understand now!" I exclaimed in my moment of the most life-changing epiphany. I was humbled by The Figure's story. I wanted to learn so much more. "Look," I pointed to moments in the 40th, 41st, 42nd, and 43rd panels. "You were horribly rejected and ridiculed to the point where You were tortured and killed. How did You deal with that?"

"Did you ever think about why I was killed? Look closely. Who killed Me? Why did they kill Me?"

I looked at the details of the panels. My heart sank with pain to see such hurtful things being done to The Figure. When I looked more closely at who the hateful people were, I was overwhelmed with a gush of surprise to realize that these were the very people who were so well educated on the 23rd panel that they should have known who The Figure was! *They* were supposed to know! Their entire life's purpose was to introduce others to The Figure!

"Wait!" I said with incredulity. "How did they *not* know who You were? They got it all wrong!"

"Like I mentioned, Anna, The Antagonist has been placing doubt in those who seek understanding at *The Door*. When people seek their own interpretation to fulfill selfish desires, The Antagonist has an easier time convincing them that *I am* The Antagonist. Since it is always easier to be deceived than it is to do what it takes to gain deeper understanding, The Antagonist usually prevails."

My head started to spin. I couldn't make sense of what The Figure was telling me. Acceptance came by my side and tried to put her arm around me. She not only became more visible, but also tangible to me in that moment. I looked at the panels and tried to make connections between what I saw on *The Door* and what I experienced in the forest.

"Anna," Wisdom appeared at *The Door*. "This Truth is not understood by many. You have the opportunity to not just understand the panels, but to make sense of the forest because of them. Your purpose is to share your understanding with others. Some people have only seen *The Door* from The Antagonist's perspective; one that is rife with deception."

I heard some rustling in the trees around us as Wisdom spoke. "There is much representation of pain and strife in the panels, but look at how loved *you* are, Anna. The Figure, who is also the Carpenter of *The Door*, loved you so much that It went through all of this to show you how much It wants a relationship with you. The entire purpose of *The Door* is for you to see and know The Figure and to be known by The Figure. It is the greatest Love you will ever find."

"I thought 'learning to love myself is the greatest love of all,'" I pondered out loud.

"To know who you are is a start. To love your authentic

self," said Acceptance, putting her fingers through my blonde hair, reminding me that I have changes to make again, "gives you the opportunity to open *The Door* to the deepest, most thirst-quenching Love you will ever find. Love exists *with* connection. You can connect in that way yourself, but the greatest Love does not end with you being alone, in love with yourself."

I looked at *The Door*. I started to see myself as part of The Figure's story. I vacillated between experiencing extreme humility and extreme love all at once. I can't believe that I lived in the forest for so long and never knew these things about it. Zooming out for a bird's eye view of *The Door* after looking at the intricacies of all the panels helped me understand The Figure's story better. The Truth about the forest was clearer to me now. This life I am living here is not about me. It is just a stage. It is more about my role in The Figure's story, not The Figure's role in mine. I felt like a secret had been revealed to me! When I had that thought, I remembered that I was not done with the journey. The Secret Cave awaited me.

"Anna, I am going to prepare the way to The Secret Cave. I'll meet you there," said Fear, her belly was quite plump now. I could see it more clearly as Insecurity, slightly visible now, clung and pulled back tufts of Fear's dress.

I waved goodbye to them and then turned my attention to the complexity and beauty of *The Door*. So many thoughts flooded my mind that one would think that my thirst for understanding was quenched, but all I could do was ask more questions. I ironically became thirstier.

"You carved this so that I would know how loved I am? You built *The Door* to share with everyone in the forest how loved they are? Is this what Your Story is about?" I asked The Figure.

The Figure held out Its wounded hands, and extended Its arms welcoming me to be held. I accepted the invitation.

"You needed to know how loved you are before you went into The Secret Cave to confront Shame and Guilt. You will not be alone in this battle, even though it is *your* battle to win," I heard The Figure whisper in my ear as It held me in an embrace. "Just remember how loved you are, Anna," It said as It let go of the embrace to remind me of the wounds in Its hands.

"It is time," Acceptance urged as she extended her hand toward the path, inviting me to progress on my journey with her by my side. "You have the information and understanding you need to make sense of what you will find in The Secret Cave."

"...and you have us to help you," Wisdom added.

This time, I extended my hands. The Figure held one, Wisdom held the other, and Acceptance held Wisdom's other hand as we all walked and talked together during our journey to The Secret Cave.

The Secret Cave

When we arrived at the entrance, Fear greeted us with a calming smile. She looked at me as a proud mother would look at a daughter who was about to graduate. Then, she looked at The Figure. They nodded at each other, and Fear's disposition became serious. A child ran up to Fear and wrapped her arms around Fear's legs. Her eyes lit up when she looked up at me and smiled.

"Hello there!" I said to the child. "Who are you?"

She giggled and held Fear's legs tighter, burying her head in the tufts of Fear's dress.

"Anna," said Fear, "This is Faith. She is my daughter. She has grown quickly since the time you saw me pregnant with her."

"Was that why you were rubbing your stomach and why it was so much larger last time I saw you? I wondered about that, but I didn't want to be rude and ask you about it!"

Fear and I let out a laugh, and she continued to share, "When you and I first met, Faith was just beginning to grow Inside. Throughout your journey, you have nurtured us through her birth by understanding *The Door*. After you fully understood the message of *The Door*, I gave birth to her, and she is now growing into a lovely little being. She has so much potential, and your work in The Secret Cave will enhance her growth even more. I look forward to seeing the woman she becomes, and the two of you will eventually become close friends."

I leaned down to talk to Faith. She looked at me with the most beautiful, sparkling eyes. I couldn't get enough of the way the light was captured inside of her pupils, almost like a stained-glass window of a church.

Fear began to speak again, "Anna, it is time for you to help her grow. As you have learned here in the forest, growth comes with some pain. Look at nature to understand. The butterfly struggles out of the chrysalis; the seed bursts through its shell and pushes up through the dirt; the body aches when bones and skin elongate. The same is true for our minds and our hearts. We struggle, burst, and ache when we grow mentally and emotionally."

"Why is it that growth and pain go together?" I asked.

"Anna, do you ever think about why I chose the crown of thorns as My helmet in the battle? My pain was not just in My hands and feet: where I went and what I did. It was also in My mind. Do you ever wonder why the sword pierced My side where My heart had already stopped beating? The source of pain was there, too. To symbolically reveal that I have felt and known their pain, I bled from and have scars in all areas where most people carry their scars from their splinters: those places where memories of hurt remain until we extract them and let those places heal. I did not shy away from the pain. I did not numb the pain. I leaned into the pain and experienced it to show how much I love *everyone* in the forest," explained The Figure.

"Did You need to go that far just to show people Love?" I asked.

"I did. No one can ever tell Me that I do not understand them."

"Empathy is one of the greatest ways to awaken, experience, and show Love," a voice from The Secret Cave shared this epiphany.

"Is Love still asleep?" I asked.

"She is resting, Anna. Once she awakens, she will be very

busy," said Hope.

"Well, hello there! I didn't see you sneak up on us!" I said, as I embraced Hope.

"I heard you calling me, and I am at your service, Anna."

"With all of you here, I don't see how my experience in The Secret Cave could be all that bad!"

Fear, Acceptance, Hope, Wisdom, and little Faith looked at The Figure, who was holding Its crown of thorns.

"This crown serves a symbolic purpose in My story, but it serves as a useful tool in your part of My story if you will allow it to do what it is meant to do here in the forest," The Figure explained.

"What do I need to do with it?" I asked.

"Look at your hands," Wisdom directed.

I did as she told me to do and saw that my hands had multiple splinters buried under my skin. "Where did these come from?" I asked. I never noticed them before.

"Before you enter Inside The Secret Cave, your eyes need to see Outside from a new perspective. Your perspective has already shifted because you were willing to stand here at the opening, and you are getting prepared to go deeper Inside. There are many hidden agendas and covert experiences that happen in the forest. You cannot see them as easily because your perspective is not focused on seeing things beyond your expectation." Wisdom ran her fingers over the splinters as she explained, "Every time someone did something to hurt you or you did something to hurt someone else, an invisible splinter was buried in your hand. Do you remember how the shards of glass from The Mere Ore Forest trees cut into your finger? When everyone was freed from the trees, you were still left with shards of splintered glass inside your hands. The people were set free, but you kept invisible reminders of all the hurt here in your hands. We can help you with these now-visible splinters. Just like surgery, it will take inflicting temporary pain to relieve you of *this* perpetual pain. The things you see Inside of The Secret Cave will also cause you pain. To prepare for the Inside pain, we are going to work through the Outside pain first."

I clenched my fists to prevent Wisdom from touching them, but then I felt the little splinters piercing my nerves. I opened my hands again and faced the fact that the splinters were there. I could not ignore them now that I saw them. The more I tried to look away or hide them, the more deeply I felt the pain that they caused.

Acceptance put her arms around me again.

"Every time hurt came into your story, a splinter formed here," Wisdom reminded me as she touched my hands. I felt the sting of each splinter as Wisdom continued, "and every time you ventured down a path that was not yours to travel, the splinters slipped into your soles," she continued explaining as she bent down and traced the splinters under the skin of each of my feet. "Now that you know they are there, they will continue to haunt and hurt you until you remove them."

"How do I remove them?" I asked, not really wanting to know the answer.

Wisdom looked down at the crown of thorns. She unraveled the crown and put one of the blood-stained thorns in between her fingers. "May I show you?"

"This is going to hurt more than I realize, isn't it?" I asked, absolutely reluctant to the idea of more pain, but desperately wanting to be rid of the splinters.

Anna Marie Savino

"It will hurt for a while, but it is the only way to make this particular pain stop hurting incessantly," Wisdom reminded me.

I put my palms up and stared at my trembling hands. I thought of times someone hurt me with the things they did. I thought of times I hurt others because of the things I did. I thought about the times I hurt The Figure and caused the scars on Its hands, feet, head, and side. Acceptance tilted her head toward me and looked me in the eyes. Knowing what Acceptance was communicating to me, I turned my glace back over to Wisdom.

"Go ahead. Get it over with," I begged Wisdom. She took the blood-stained thorn and inserted it into my hand. The pointed tip pierced above the skin where the smallest splinter laid buried. The first prick stung. The sharpness dug deeper, and I winced.

"Breathe, Anna. Look, it is coming out. Look at it. See it for what it is," Wisdom reassured me. "Can you hear what it is revealing?"

I looked down. As the splinter emerged, words floated from the splinter into the air like smoke. I could hear the words as they evaporated. My ears felt like they were breathing in the sound of each word. As I breathed, I could feel the words on the wind entering my lungs. Then, I exhaled a toxic smoke, cloudy and thick. I coughed, and soot sprayed from my breath. "What is happening to me?" I asked, barely being able to breathe.

"You have created dark walls Inside by the smoke from Hell Fires, Anna. What you experienced Outside has affected Inside. Before we go into the cave, we need to take out these splinters and teach you how to breathe freely. If you don't learn this now, going Inside of The Secret Cave will suffocate you."

85

I took a deep breath in; coughed more soot; looked at The Figure, Fear, Hope, and little Faith; leaned into Acceptance's inviting arms; opened my palm toward Wisdom, and said, "Keep going."

"As you wish, Anna," Wisdom said, and she used another thorn from the crown to extract the next splinter, and the next, and the next.

The splinter removal started with the surface splinters. I had not felt pain like that in my hands before. I continued to breathe as Wisdom removed more splinters. By the time she was digging out the splinters that were lodged deeper into my skin, the process became more tolerable. I learned to breathe through the pain, and less soot emerged from my exhalation.

When Wisdom was finished, my hands were a bloody mess. The Figure came close to me. "May I?" The Figure asked. I nodded and then felt Its hands over mine. Light emerged from The Figure's scars, and a soothing coolness tickled my wounds. When The Figure removed Its hands, all of the blood was gone, and my hands were clean.

"How did you do that?" I asked.

"You'll see," replied The Figure.

I looked at The Figure with frustration, to which It responded, "It is too much to explain now. You will know when you are ready to know."

"Why did that need to happen before I went into The Secret Cave?" I asked.

"You cannot confront The Secrets when you are holding onto so much pain," Wisdom explained.

I looked down at my feet. "Do we need to do the same thing to my feet?"

"Not yet," answered Wisdom, as she took some of the thorns from the crown and placed them in some of the blank spaces of my necklace. "You will need these later. Are you ready to go into The Secret cave now, Anna?" She looked down at my necklace, then up at me again and smiled.

I tucked the necklace back under the collar of my dress, took a deep breath in, and exhaled. No soot. "Yes," I breathed in and out again, "I'm ready."

Fear gestured her arm toward the opening of the cave. Hope, Acceptance, and little Faith went in before me. The Figure walked beside me, holding my healed hand in Its scarred hand. Fear followed us into the darkness.

"Well, well, well, look who finally showed up," a disdainful voice echoed in the darkness.

"I'm here. You know who I am. Who are you?" I asked.

A match ignited and lit the wick of a hand-held candle. I could see that I found Shame and Guilt, hiding in the dark of The Secret Cave; their faces illuminated by the tiny, flickering fire in front of them. They were the ones who started most of the Hell Fires Inside.

Shame smiled, turned around, and silently led the way deeper into the cave. The rest of us followed her, with Guilt guiding the back of our line.

The Figure was with me in the dark, still walking beside me, holding my hand. It whispered, "I AM with you, Anna. Do not be afraid."

"Fear is my friend now," I reminded myself while whispering those words to The Figure.

"She has another name when she is your friend. You can

continue to call her Fear at times, but in this state, she is better known as Respect."

For now, Fear walked beside us as Respect, with Faith now in her arms, and we all followed Shame until we came to a place that echoed with moaning and sobbing. "Where are these sounds coming from?" I asked.

"Those are The Secrets, Anna," Guilt answered as she caught up to the rest of us. "They have been hidden here in this cave, locked up, and guarded by Shame and me. We keep them hidden for you, but allow them to remain alive and," she paused to smirk, "well-nourished."

I took a deep breath and could feel the thickness of the air around me penetrating my freshly cleaned lungs. The cave smelled like rotting corpses: decay, mold, and sickness. "What do I need to do in here?" I asked, ready to do what it took to be able to leave as quickly as possible.

"You can leave now if you'd like," Shame said, seeming eager to have me choose that option.

"No. What do I need to do while I am here?"

"It won't be easy..." Shame started to say.

"I am not afraid of something being difficult, Shame."

"That's not what I have seen, Anna," she mocked. "Over here," Shame pointed to a prison cell and put the flickering fire of the candle in front of it to illuminate what was Inside, "are your Cowardly Secrets: your lies, your running away so quickly when things become... difficult." She let out a subtle, yet deeply fiendish laugh. "Do you want a closer look?" As Shame asked this, Guilt walked up to the cell, wrapped one of her hands around one of the bars of the door, and wiggled it. Collective shrieking filled my ears. I could not clearly see what was Inside.

At first, I just wanted to run away, but that is apparently what created this place. It was time to do the opposite of what I was comfortable doing to fix a situation. This time, I needed to fight the urge to run away. I felt empowered by The Figure's hand in mine.

"Yes," I said, determined and ready.

"Anna, I am here with you too," whispered the voice of a teenage girl.

"I can't see you very well. Who are you?"

"Faith," she answered, while taking the hand not occupied by The Figure's into hers and giving me a reassuring squeeze. I didn't know that Faith was capable of growing that quickly!

With the candle in her hand, Shame lit three more candle wicks at the front of the cell. Everything was illuminated in the cave. Upon seeing the light, The Cowardly Secrets all shrieked again and backed out of sight.

"The Lion! The Lying! The Lion!" they all screamed, repeatedly. "The Lying! The Lion! The Lying!"

I looked around me and didn't see a lion. They must have been talking about The Figure. I once thought It was a lion, but I couldn't understand why they were screaming about lying. I wondered if there was something else in the cave that I couldn't see in the dark spaces of The Secret Cave.

I could barely see the Cowardly Secrets because they retreated far into the back corners of the cell. Their shrieking started to unnerve me, and my desire to run out of the cave grew stronger. I looked at The Figure and Faith in the firelight of the darkness. They reassured me, nodding toward the cell entrance.

"Stop!" I said calmly in the direction of the cell. The voices stopped. "Why are you screaming? There is nothing to be afraid of. We're here to set you free."

Shame laughed. Guilt remained guarding the cell door.

I let go of the hands of The Figure and Faith, gave them a hug, and walked toward Shame and Guilt. I knew that The Figure and Faith would still be with me, but that I needed my hands to do the work that fulfilled the purpose I had in The Secret Cave.

Walking over to the entrance of the cell, I could feel Fear's presence behind me. I whispered, "Fear, thank you for trying to protect me. I need you to go stand with The Figure and Faith. I finally know that I am not alone. You all have given me the strength I need to do what I came here to do." Fear respectfully walked over to The Figure and Faith. They all stood together, watching me.

Shame didn't laugh this time. Guilt backed away from the entrance of the cell door.

I walked up to where Guilt had stood and put my face through two of the bars of the cell. "Come here so that I can see you," I commanded.

"You don't want to see us, Anna. No, no; we are not ready for you. You are not ready for us. You are still afraid," they all tried to warn me in unison.

"I am not afraid of you," I replied.

Shame didn't move. She couldn't move. Guilt backed herself into a dark corner where she could no longer be seen.

"I'm sorry that I kept you in here for so long. I am ready to see you. I am ready to hear you. I am ready to let you out of this place," I said, projecting my voice into the cell.

One Cowardly Secret cautiously, yet bravely, made its way to meet me at the bars. She was one of the ugliest beings I had seen up to this point. Her hair- what was left of it- was sporadically lifted from the scalp, as if she had been purposefully pulling it out bit by bit. She came close to the bar and looked me in the eyes. Her eyes were so tired, as if she had never known what it was like to close them. "Help me," she begged, as she stretched out her gnarled and bruised hands through the bars.

I began to cry; my tears landed on her outstretched hands. I buried my face in her hands and wept. The pain I felt was not like the pain from the removal of the splinters. There was a piercing pain deep within myself carried up from my stomach, through my heart, and into my mind; all of the parts of my physical being that kept me alive were now experiencing deep pain traveling through them until the pain exited through the tears in my eyes. "I'm...so sorry for... not letting you out of here sooner," I cried. The Cowardly Secret stroked my hair- enviously, I suppose- wetting it with my own tears. She took my weeping face in her hands again for a while longer. Then, she removed her tear-soaked hands away from my face and gestured to the others, summoning them that it was safe to come out and show themselves. Another Cowardly Secret came into view. She was just a child, but she was more grotesque than the first. I shuddered but stayed where I was; tears still dripping from my eyes. The first Secret took the tears that fell in her hands and wiped the grime off the face of the second Secret.

Another Cowardly Secret saw what was happening and emerged from the dark. More and more came into the light of the fire, and the water from my tears were being used to wash away the dirt and dismay. By the time all the Cowardly Secrets revealed themselves, I could see that all of them looked like me at the age that they all came to The Secret Cave. Some were me as a child; some were me as a teenager; while others looked similar to the way I looked just before I met The Figure; before The Well crumbled. Only one of The Secrets looked similar to how I looked at that moment. She reached through the bars and grabbed my necklace out from under the collar of my dress. I almost stopped her, until I noticed that, between her right index finger and thumb, she held the key that was shaped from Forgiveness's stone embedded into necklace. "Let us out of here now," she demanded with a smile.

Shame and Guilt were hiding together in the corner of the cave, out of sight.

I took the key and found the lock that secured the door to the cell. The Cowardly Secrets were set free. Three of them took the lit candles from the entrance to their now-opened cell and placed them in front of the cells that contained Sexual Secrets, Abuse Secrets, and Identity Secrets. The Cowardly Secrets, now empowered, encouraged the other Secrets to come into view and reveal themselves to me.

I was in the cave for a year and a half, talking to each Secret until they were all free.

During my time in the cave, there were moments when I needed to take a break from conversing with The Secrets to be held by The Figure and Faith, who had now become a young lady. Fear came by my side occasionally, as Shame and Guilt stirred in their dark corner shouting words of discouragement. Sometimes, I would listen to them and The Secrets ran back into their opened cell.

It took Faith's reassurance to help me continue what I went Inside of the cave to do. She grew quickly in The Secret Cave. I learned that My Secrets were not as frightening and disgusting as Shame and Guilt made them appear. With each new enlightenment in the dark Secret Cave, my tears and time with The Secrets transformed their distorted appearance.

They surrounded me in delight, celebrating their liberation; their being known. Their moaning and sobbing transformed into harmonious singing; their song similar to the one I heard from the bird trapped when The Well crumbled.

"Well, hello Anna," said Freedom. "I'm so proud of you!"

"Freedom! It has been so long since I've seen you! Why do you keep disappearing?" I asked.

"There are times when you will be able to see me, and times when I will be here, but you will not see me."

"It is so nice to see you now," I said, as I embraced Freedom.

"Anna, we have something for you," the first Cowardly Secret said to me, and each Secret handed me a small stone to put in my necklace. *How could something so frightening turn into something so beautiful?* I wondered.

"That is the nature of things," said Wisdom, answering the question she read in my mind.

"Wisdom! Look!" I pointed at my necklace.

"Anna, it is becoming more and more beautiful with each part of your journey," she commented.

I walked over to The Figure and Faith. Fear must have left sometime during the celebration with The Secrets. Guilt and Shame had disappeared.

"Look at you, Anna!" Faith said as she hugged me and then pulled back to look at the necklace. She was now my height and had almost caught up to my current age.

"Is there anything else I need to do while we are here?" I asked.

The Figure handed me a pen that was shaped like a pickaxe. "It is time for you to axe what you have been doing here by picking words that will tear down the dark walls of this Shame-created cave. Write away."

As I accepted the pen from The Figure, I knew exactly what The Figure wanted me to do. I took the pen and began writing on the walls of the cave. I wrote furiously.

My pen scratched over the walls of the cave in sweeping motions, chipping away at the sides, little by little. The more I wrote, the more the pieces of the walls of the cave flew away into the air and landed on the ground near my feet.

I wrote:

I am blessed by the ability to learn from my mistakes. I am thankful for the friends that have unconditionally loved me. I have a mother who is willing to be lovingly honest with me. I have a father who provides safety and security for me. I have a job that gives me opportunities to learn and grow as an individual while being able to help others. I learned what it means to take care of myself financially for now....

The more the pen scratched affirmations of gratitude on the wall, the more the darkness on the wall crumbled around me. Bright, colorful light started to shine through the cracks in the walls. It inspired me to keep writing.

I am blessed by The Secrets being known. I am thankful for the crown of thorns because I had so many splinters to remove. I have The Figure's love. I have ambitions to share my story with others. I have Freedom, who helps me take time to make better choices with my experience. I learned what it means to live with Fear as a friend...as Respect.

The more the pen scratched affirmations of gratitude on the wall, the more light I saw. The more that the colors pierced the darkness, the more I wanted to write. I wrote until the walls of

The Secret Cave crumbled, like The Well, and revealed that I was in a place where the walls and ceiling were made with stained-glass windows.

"Some things need to crumble and fall apart in order to see how beautiful they are underneath," Wisdom claimed. "Wasn't this worth all of that pain?"

I looked around dumbfounded at the immense beauty that had been covered and unseen by my own warped perspective; by cave-like walls lined with smoke from Hell Fires to hide My Secrets in the dark. I basked in the colors around me; I felt Hope and Acceptance appear in the cave near me. We sat in the light for a long time, paying attention to the details of the windows and the stories that they told with each perfectly crafted scene. They were the stories of My Secrets set free in a beautiful light.

"Anna, it is time to go back to The Swamp." Acceptance stood up and started walking toward the opening of the cave.

"I was just beginning to feel peaceful, calm, and happy here." My mood changed. "Why is it that when I finish one major task, I need to leave the celebration of it to begin a new task? When does this all end?"

"It really doesn't end, Anna. Each difficult time will end with a beautiful moment. You will learn to enjoy those moments more deeply because you know how fleeting they are," Wisdom said as she observed the beauty of the stained-glass pictures around us. "You have been training for the moment you are about to experience. Everything you have learned up to this point will be useful in the next battle."

"This next battle will be the most difficult for you, Anna," The Figure shared. "You will have trouble; you will have more pain; but you do not need to worry. Remember the 4th section of the 40th panel of *The Door*? I have been through this type of battle, and I have already won. Use that as a reminder for how to fight. You will become thirsty again, but anything other than the water Wisdom or I give you will be tainted and will make you sick. The Swamp taints the water of the forest. It is time for you to go to The Swamp so that you can confront The Queen. Once that happens, the murky water of The Swamp will change and can be used as a source for The Well. Remember that when The Antagonist tries to tempt and deceive you."

"I am going to meet The Antagonist?"

The Figure and Wisdom looked at each other and then back at me in pity. They knew what was ahead of me on my journey.

I confronted the people trapped in the trees of The Mere Ore Forest, freed The Secrets, and conquered darkness with gratitude. These were all smaller battles within themselves, but they were also the training ground for the bigger battle. The fact that I accomplished these steps made me a threat to The Antagonist.

"You will not meet The Antagonist alone, Anna. I will be there with you. I also have this for you," The Figure said and laid a heavy bag at my still-splintered feet. "This is from the 6th section of the 49th panel of *The Door*."

"This heavy bag is for me?"

"Yes. Open it, observe it, and then put on what you find inside as Armor for your battle, Anna," The Figure commanded.

I opened the bag. All I saw were words. "These are just words. How am I supposed to wear these as Armor?"

"Anna, The Antagonist cannot be defeated with physical objects. These words represent The Armor you need to use to protect yourself."

"Teach me," I requested, inviting The Figure to guide me.

The Figure took out the word "Truth" and tied it around my waist. The phrase "The Protection of Right Living" covered my chest and "Good News of Peace" wrapped my splintered feet. The Figure took A Word from Its head and placed it on mine. Then, The Figure handed me a sword with the word "Ezer" etched in its blade. After placing all the Armor Words on me, I learned how to use them.

It took weeks of focused training before I felt as though I understood how to properly wear and use the Armor Words.

"You are well-prepared for the battle," The Figure said, and we walked together with The Emotions back to The Swamp.

Sparrow's Well

Bull's "I"

Wisdom and The Figure were on protective defense when we arrived back at the edge of The Swamp, where I last saw The Queen.

"Anna, The Antagonist is wily and will do whatever it takes to get you to succumb to The Queen's demands. She answers to The Antagonist and has the power to deceive you in a way that will seem logical, even if that choice will eventually have adverse outcomes for you. It will be difficult, but you can resist. *Trust Me*," The Figure warned and requested.

I remembered how The Figure helped me conquer Shame and Guilt's power over me. From that experience, I learned that, when I want to retreat from what I know is good for me, I needed to take the opposite action.

I didn't like the thought of being under The Queen's control. I knew that listening to her advice would just keep me masked and hidden under lies.

I was tired, but I still had fight within me. The moment I recognized that within myself, I saw The Queen walking toward me. I didn't waste time before confronting her.

"Everything you have done to help me has had the reverse effect! I do not want your help anymore! Please just go away!" I screamed at her.

"You can't get rid of me. I am a part of you. If you kill me, you kill yourself. If you silence me, you silence yourself," The Queen responded ominously. "You can't get rid of me, Anna. You are stuck with me, so you might as well accept that I will always control you. Always." She flung her head back and laughed, her hair flying behind her and bouncing with each cackle.

Then, I had an epiphany that changed everything. My hair was the very thing that she has used to control me. This was the first of many things that she used to bandage my hatred for myself. It was time to rip off the Band-Aid that attempted to cover-- but would never heal-- the toxic illness in my heart. The addiction to validation needed to go next. I also needed to say goodbye to the people who paid attention to me the way I needed them to because they only wanted the illusion of me as badly as I needed their attention.

I didn't need my hair to be a certain way to be accepted. I didn't need the constant validation. I didn't need inauthentic relationships that were all talk and no action. Once I found that undeniable connection, those things I thought I needed became Idle amusements. Those Idles ran toward The Queen, seeking to be rescued from my desire to eliminate them.

At the same time, The Figure appeared with Wisdom, Fear, and Acceptance. They all stood back to let me make my decisions.

I reached up into the roots coming out of my scalp and started to pull out the pieces that were not naturally attached to my head.

"What are you doing?" The Queen looked slightly worried while trying to maintain her powerful disposition.

"Just keep talking. Tell me how I am nothing without you and how much I need you to survive," I responded while pulling more of the fake parts attached to my head and letting them drop to the ground. I kept my eyes on The Figure.

"Stop! What are you doing?" The Queen's feet began to sink

into The Swamp.

"No questions. Just keep talking."

Another piece of hair dropped to the ground. My eyes were locked on The Figure's loving expression. The Queen was trying to speak, but she could only mouth the words she was trying to say. No sound came from her mouth. "What's that? I couldn't hear you. You are going to need to speak louder if I am going to be affected by your words, *my* Queen." The more I mocked her and undid what she had done, the more motionless she became and the deeper she sank into her self-created swamp.

I was surprised by how much I had to remove in order to take away everything she changed about me. I kept pulling out the pieces that didn't belong. One piece after the other fell until every piece of the mask of manipulated and fabricated identity crumbled into unrecognizable pieces—like The Well.

As that identity was falling apart, other parts of me mended back together. I felt a strength I had never known before. It was more solid than the feeling I had after my time in The Mere Ore Forest and The Secret Cave. I began building that strength through all my experiences since The Figure met me at my weakest moment in the forest.

Here at the edge of The Swamp with my Armor of Words and my experience with The Emotions and The Figure, I was no longer under The Queen's control, and she couldn't run away this time.

I saw Carelessness, with the remote in a sloshing glass of water, running to the sinking queen.

"Here! I brought you what you need!" it said, fumbling clumsily.

"You," I turned my attention to Carelessness and took the

remote from inside the water glass, "no longer need to bother with this. This remote control is broken. It is useless." I tossed the remote into The Swamp. Carelessness was done trying to fix things, but it still ran to The Queen to try to help. The Queen grabbed onto Carelessness. As Carelessness attempted to help The Queen, they both sank deeper into The Swamp. When they sunk so low that their arms were buried and useless, I walked over to The Queen and took the crown off her head. Her appearance changed. The mask was gone. She looked exactly like me now. I bent down next to her face and said, "You no longer rule here. Your rules no longer apply."

"Is that so?" asked a creature who suddenly appeared and smirked as it took three arrows from a satchel. A snake slithered up to its feet and circled it in protection.

"Ego, I guess you are no longer The Queen here," the creature said.

I was taken aback and had to think about the implications of what I just heard. After contemplating all the experiences that I had with 'The Queen,' it made sense that she would be Ego. Luckily for me, she was stuck in the mud and no longer had control over me.

I felt a sense of relief at this revelation until I saw that the creature with the snakes at its feet lit one of the arrows on fire and put it into the bow, pulled back, and said, "Did The Figure really think that *words* would make a suitable Armor for you? You poor dear, you have been deceived this whole time. The Figure *wanted* me to defeat you. That is why you are here. Ego is stuck in the mud, and you don't have *real* Armor. All of your original defenses have been stripped away from you, and I am more easily able to take over now."

As it aimed the arrow at me, another creature was coming toward me from the opposite side of The Swamp. It was beastly, like a giant bull, and growled as it galloped toward me. It had sharp fangs, and its eyes pierced into me, much like I imagined the arrow would if it was released.

I looked over at the tip of the arrow that was waving at me, mocking me with its flickering, hand-like flames. As my right hand began to rise instinctually to either wave back or block the impending arrow, it brushed against the scabbard that was attached to the belt word "Truth." I pulled out my sword. Light reflected off the blade. I looked down at the word, "Ezer" and remembered my purpose. I kept the sword lit in the rays of sun that were shining through fog that blurred my vision of The Swamp.

I could barely see the beastly creature as it progressed quickly over the murky waters toward me, and I didn't know which of my two opponents I was supposed to defend myself against.

Each time the beastly creature's legs met the muddy ground, I could feel the ground beneath me shake, slowly and violently, and I had difficulty remaining balanced. When the beastly creature finally caught up to me, I tried to ward it off with the sword, but it was stronger than I was at that moment. It pounced on top of me so forcefully that the sword fell out of my hand. The beastly creature growled directly into my right ear.

I wrestled, almost defenseless, trying to get back to the sword that glistened on the ground. I tried to move, but I was paralyzed in the beastly creature's grip. One of its paws raised up to strike my chest. It growled again, this time, in my left ear.

My first thought was that this was the end of the battle for me; this beastly creature was about to end my life. Then, I remembered what The Figure said about not being alone. In the blink of an eye, the memories of my journey flashed before me. I remembered all the souvenirs that I collected on my necklace.

In defense, I did the opposite of what I would have usually done in a moment like that. Instead of trying to pull away, I moved my chest directly into the beastly creature's paw. The dainty intricacies on my necklace pieced the metacarpal, and the beastly creature shrieked back with a painful yelp. The thorns from the crown must have pierced the creature's paw. I stood up and looked at the bleeding creature and then down at the sword, glistening brighter than ever.

I heard a piercing scream and looked up to see that the first arrow was just released by the other creature. I quickly averted my gaze to The Light reflecting off the sword. The Light shone on The Figure, and I could see that it was motioning for me to kneel. When I did, the arrow flew straight over my head and landed in the beastly creature behind me.

"No! Doubt!" Carelessness let out a helpless, childish squeal. "Doubt is wounded!" it said to Ego, who was shoulder deep in The Swamp next to her.

"Doubt! You'll be ok. Pull through! Get up and show your strength!" Ego yelled from her paralyzed state.

I didn't recognize that the beastly creature was Doubt until it was wounded and helpless. I was able to get closer to see what it looked like without getting attacked by it. I saw it before, but it looked different every time I encounter it. At that moment, with a fire arrow stuck in its side, it looked tired and meek.

Doubt looked at Ego and sighed. Then, it directed its attention to Carelessness and began to speak. "Tell Pride... that... I am wounded. I'm not dead...yet, but, for a while...I will be as useless as you are without your remote. Please, get someone to take me away from here."

At the moment Doubt surrendered in defeat, Faith, with the beauty and strength of a mature woman, appeared at The Swamp to carry away the giant, bullish creature. The other creature screamed at Faith, "Get away from here before I wound you, too!"

Another arrow was lit on fire and placed it into the bow. The creature turned to me and mocked, "You don't even know how to use the sword! If all you do is use it to blind others when fighting, you are weak. I know you are better than that, but you will never see your worth as a fighter if you don't know how to use your weapons correctly. Come on, try and kill me with *that* sword. Let's see how strong you really are."

I got up from the ground, took the sword from its resting place, and held it up to reflect Light back toward the creature so it would stay blind. The Word in the sword was the only thing plainly visible, as The Light started to transform the creature into a ghost, opposite from the way Acceptance appeared to me.

I remembered a song that I used to sing while gathering flowers in the forest. The line "...and the things of [the forest] will grow strangely dim in The Light..." is true. I realized that *this* sword's purpose was not to be used to hurt people! It was just meant to defend its possessor by reflecting the Light.

"Anna, you forget that I am part of you. When you hurt me, you hurt yourself. I am not going anywhere, and neither are you," the creature's voice said as faintly as its figure was evaporating. "It is your destiny to stay here with me in The Swamp," it said as it aimed for my heart.

"Who are you?" I asked. I thought I knew the answer, so I

ask a more specific question immediately afterwards, "Are you The Antagonist?"

"My reputation must have preceded me," was all it said in reply. The snake around its feet moved more erratically.

I held up the sword trying to use The Light to blind it.

My efforts were partially effective, as the creature released a second flame-tipped arrow that missed my heart, but it hit my face. The arrow hit in the space just between my upper lip and my nose. The pain was so sharp that I fell to the ground, and the sword flew out of my hand. All I could do was think about the pain. I tried to speak, but the pain burned so deeply that I could only make grunting sounds. I pulled out the arrow and tried to form my mouth into an O to blow out the fire that seared my skin. I couldn't move my mouth. I threw the arrow to the side and put my face into the tufts of my dress to blot the blood from my wound.

As I hung my head down, blood dripped from my face onto the ground. I blotted it again. Each time that I touched my wound to blot the blood away, I winced and felt weaker.

The sword twinkled in the sunlight three feet away from me. I was so close to it but felt so paralyzed by the pain that I didn't retrieve it.

Each time I breathed, I was reminded of my wound and of the pain it was causing me. The Antagonist wounded the main source of my connection with others. It got two birds with one arrow: In its attempt to pierce my heart, it instead wounded my ability to speak and, in doing so, blocked off my heart.

As I continued to hang my head, two feet appeared in view next to my feet. I lifted my head up to see if The Antagonist finally came close enough to defeat me, but the two feet belonged to Silence. The Antagonist, content with its victory, sat quietly nearby.

Silence and I sat together for a long time. I wanted so badly to communicate, but I had to heal first. I remembered that I had a pen in my necklace. I took it out and began to write on whatever I could find around me that would accept the ink of the pen. I wrote everything that happened to me in the forest since The Well crumbled up to that very moment in my journey.

Tears welled up in my eyes, dripped down my face, and seeped into my wound. Silence held me tightly as I cried. I didn't know if I enjoyed being held by her, or if I wanted to break free. Her grip was somewhat painful, but so was trying to speak. All I could do was cry.

To some, crying is a sign of weakness, but I learned that I was stronger because I allowed myself to feel. It hurt to cry, but the more I cried, the less pain I felt when Silence held me. The more I cried, the faster my wound healed. I continued to write through the tears because beautiful words emerged from my pen when my mouth couldn't speak.

A warm presence came close as I was hunched over writing, still held by Silence. I was pleasantly surprised to see Faith. She held the sword as she was standing tall looking over me.

"Anna, you are going to be ok. This pain will not last. Feel it. Trust that it has something to teach you," she said as she handed me the sword. "It is time for Silence to let go now."

Silence never said anything the entire time she held me, and as quietly as she came, she drifted away.

I tried to speak to Faith. It took me time to finally say, "Thank you. I have missed you being here. Please don't go away again."

"Anna, that part is all up to you. Let me help you with your battle. You cannot do this on your own."

"I'm so tired. My body is weary, my feet are still splintered, and my mouth is still healing from the arrow. Please help me."

Faith extended her hand to me. I accepted the invitation and stood up with her help.

The Antagonist must have heard me speaking again, because it instantly stood up in its ghostly state and moved closer to where Faith and I were standing. It took the last arrow from its quiver and lit it on fire. It didn't put it in the bow this time. It waved the fire around in front of us.

"You have seen what these arrows can do. The last time you fought me, you were defeated and under Silence's care for a long time. I don't think you want to see what I am capable of doing to you next time." It paused, changed its disposition from disdain to delight. "I'll tell you what, Anna. I'm tired of fighting with you. I don't want to hurt you, because when you hurt, I hurt. How about we just agree to become friends? We can stop fighting, and I can give you everything that will make your heart happy again. I can rebuild The Well for you."

It was right about one thing: I was tired. I didn't want to fight anymore, and I was almost desperate enough to do whatever it took to just make the pain and struggle go away. I was ready to extend my hand to make a deal with The Antagonist, when, out of the corner of my eye, I saw the words of story I had just written.

I remembered what The Figure did for me. I remembered that it was under The Antagonist's orders that Ego gave me a makeover. I remembered how hard it was to become myself again, ripping apart the manipulated identity to be who I truly am.

I came this far, and I didn't want all of what I had just gone through to end in vain. As if sensing my need for her, Faith gave me the sword. I knew it was time to confront The Antagonist. "It took me a long time to undo what you have done," I told the creature.

"Anna, believe it or not, you are the one who made those decisions. Don't blame me for what you allowed me to do. Everything I have done has been to help you, not to hurt you. The forest is such a scary place, and if you don't look a certain way, act a certain way, or say the right things, you won't survive," The Antagonist said, still waving its flaming arrow around as it spoke. Then, it pointed the arrow at me, again directly in line with my heart. "I have helped you survive this whole time. All the times people loved and accepted you were because *I* helped you. *I* was the one who told you how beautiful you are. *I* was the one who made you flirtatiously clever. *I* was the one who pushed you to work so hard and become the success that you are. Just trust in *me*, and *I* will lead you safely through this forest." The creature tried to make peace as it handed the flaming arrow to another ghostly creature who appeared next to it. Certainty held out its hand to accept the flaming arrow. The Antagonist stretched out its hand to me, as if it was ready to shake on a deal.

The light from the fire illuminated Certainty's faintly visible, yet charming and alluring face. I saw that Certainty was smiling at Faith. It wasn't a friendly smile, but rather a smile that a soldier would give its enemy right before it knew that the enemy was going to be defeated.

I looked at The Antagonist's inviting hand. It looked nothing like The Figure's hand. I remembered The Figure's hands and how they were wounded to show me how loved I am. I considered the fact that, with The Antagonist, I had Certainty on my side and would know what to expect in the forest: how to act, what to say, how to make people like me. Then, I considered the fact that, with The Figure, I had Faith and *The Door*: how to love, what to prioritize, how to make life in the forest more meaningful. I believed that I could have a fascinating life with The Antagonist's help, but I trusted that The Figure's Love would continue to show me adventures beyond Certainty's capabilities. Faith was right, I couldn't do this on my own.

I felt the sword's power in my hand. I had the power to destroy The Antagonist. It was vulnerable. It was increasingly disappearing into a faint, ghostly figure. I almost felt pity for it.

Even though I could not fight The Antagonist on my own, I knew that my future was my choice. This whole time, I thought all my feelings and all my experiences were the direct result of natural circumstances. I realized that my choice is what shaped everything I experienced and everything I felt. Most of the time, I had been choosing not to choose. Indecision is a choice, and it comes with its own set of consequences. I let The Emotions and others' actions take priority over my own choice.

How could I have been so blind to not understand that choice was such a powerful gift? Without it, we are all puppets. With it, we have the chance to understand authentic desire. It was time for me to open that gift that was presented to the world in the second section of the first panel of *The Door*.

I took the sword and touched the tip of it to The Antagonist's woundless hand and then raised it to its heart. It nodded at me. Its disposition became sadistic as it commanded, "Do it. Destroy me."

"No," I replied. "I don't need to destroy you to live without you ruling everything I do. You have already been defeated by the wounds in The Figure's hands. I choose life with The Figure, and I will live the rest of my time in the forest being of service to The Figure instead of being like these creatures who are servants to you. It is time for you to go away now."

At those words, The Antagonist ran away out of sight. Certainty followed behind it with the last flaming arrow. I saw the flame die out as it was waved around aimlessly in the whispering of the wind.

I didn't need to hurt or destroy The Antagonist. I just needed to make a choice. It seemed so complexly simple and anticlimactic.

Once I made the choice, Hope, Acceptance, Faith, and The Figure came to my side. I immediately ran to The Figure and said, "I know that I am unworthy of Your Love, but you have shown me that I am *still* loved more deeply than I have ever been or will ever be loved by anyone else. All the Idles," I looked around The Swamp at all of the creatures that Ego and The Antagonist collected, "are here because The Antagonist thought that they would give me the love that You have already given me. I just couldn't see it until now." I wrapped my arms around The Figure's waist and put my head on Its chest, my right ear against Its heart and said, "I choose you."

Hope, Acceptance, and Faith jumped up and down and clapped their hands in delight. I quickly found myself in a group embrace. As we held each other, I felt my strength come back. I was no longer weary. I felt safe and content in the intimate presence of The Figure.

Sparrow's Well

Waking Up

I remembered that splinters were still in my feet.

"Walk with Me, Anna," The Figure invited, knowing what my next step was going to be.

I nodded, The Figure held my hand, and we walked toward the edge of The Swamp. The murky water rippled at our feet.

"Are we going to walk around The Swamp to the Other Side?" I asked.

"No," replied The Figure, releasing my hand and stepping halfway across The Swamp on the surface of the cloudy, mud-filled water.

"How are You doing that?" I gasped.

The Figure turned Its glance to Faith, who was standing confidently on the edge of The Swamp, silhouetted in the sunlight behind us.

"Just keep your focus on Me, and we can cross The Swamp together," The Figure invited.

My splintered foot trembled as it touched the surface of the dirty water. I took my first full step, then looked up at The Figure.

I took another step, and another, and another, until I was four steps away from the shore. The wake from the shadowy water rippled under my feet. I was doing it! I was walking to The Figure without sinking into The Swamp!

"Keep your eyes on Me, Anna," The Figure reminded me. "No need to look down. You know how to walk. Just keep putting one foot in front of the other, and we will make it to the Other Side together."

I was about two steps away from The Figure when it felt like something beneath the surface of the water of The Swamp was pulling me down. It felt like I was quickly sinking into wet sand.

"Anna, look at Me," The Figure kept saying.

The Idles appeared and were trying to pull me under the surface of the molasses-thickness of The Swamp around us. It seemed the instances when they were most active were the times when I was trying to get away from them. Apparently, The Idles still had a mind of their own, without Ego's or The Antagonist's prompting. In fact, they were less tame on their own.

Ego was paralyzed, The Antagonist fled, but The Idles were still around. *How could that be?*

"Anna, The Idles were never under Ego's or The Antagonist's control. You are the one who keeps them alive. You are their nurturer. If you come with Me across The Swamp, you will realize you don't need them, and they will no longer get their nourishment. After some time, they could cease to exist," The Figure explained, once again, reading my mind.

The Idles heard The Figure and began to use "What If?" statements to catch me and pull me under the toxic muck.

"What if The Figure isn't real?" shouted one Idle. My ankles became buried until the muddy water.

"What if The Figure can't satisfy you like I can?" smirked another Idle. I sunk further until my legs became trapped inside the mud.

"What if you will need to give up everything you worked so hard to accomplish when you get to the Other Side of The Swamp?" asked a worried Idle.

"What if you end up homeless? What if you lose friends? What if you end up alone?" as The Idles kept asking questions, I was pulled deeper into The Swamp, paralyzed up to my neck, just like Ego.

The Figure brought Faith close to me. She reverted into her child-like self. Perplexed and scared, I looked to The Figure for guidance.

"They know that I AM stronger than their 'What Ifs,' Anna," said The Figure, "but you are the one who needs to believe that. I will take care of you. You already chose Me. It is time to *trust* your choice and put it into action."

I tried to reach my hand up for The Figure's hand, but my arms were stuck below the surface of The Swamp.

The Figure asked, "Do you want My help? I AM here to help you, but I cannot make that choice for you, Anna."

I looked around at The Idles, hearing the echoes of their "What Ifs," while slowly sinking even deeper, being consumed and surrounded by diluted quicksand.

"Anna, will you *trust* Me?" The Figure asked, ready to rescue me.

I wanted to say yes, but something was preventing me. I kept looking at The Idles. Their "What Ifs" were progressively louder, and I could barely hear The Figure's voice with their screaming. I felt trapped. I couldn't focus. All I could do was worry that I would drown in The Swamp.

The Figure came closer to me and reached out for me. The more I looked at The Figure, the deeper The Idles around me began to sink into The Swamp. They knew they were about to be buried in the muddy wake of The Swamp, so they all cried out with everything they had left within them.

"Why can't You just pull me out of here?" I asked The Figure.

"You need to invite My help, Anna. I will never use force with you. Choice is a gift for both the Giver and the Receiver. You just need to keep choosing Me and putting that choice into action."

Once my shoulders became submerged, I noticed that the necklace containing all the reminders of my journey was floating in front of my face. Was my entire journey going to end this way? Did I fight all of those battles to submit to being trapped with the Idles in The Swamp? I remembered how strong I became after each part of the journey. I remembered that The Figure was the only constant. I remembered what happened when I chose The Figure over The Antagonist, and how choosing was so simple, yet so difficult to do with all the distractions and options around me.

I was done being trapped. I was done feeling helpless. I was finally ready to put my choice into action.

I redirected my focus and screamed out The Figure's name. Immediately, I felt two wounded hands pull me from The Swamp and carry me across to the Other Side.

Once I was safely on the shore of the Other Side of The Swamp, I could feel the weight and thickness of the dirt that covered me. I looked back at The Swamp, and The Idles were nowhere to be seen. A strange feeling of grief came over me. I didn't know how attached I was to the Idles until they were gone. I couldn't help but completely fall apart in both frustration with myself as well as relief for The Figure's help.

Once again, tears flooded out of my eyes, hitting and softening the hardened parts of thick mud that covered me from the shoulders down. The Figure let me cry and handed me a full cup from which to drink to replenish all that I had lost with my seemingly endless crying. I continued to weep until my eyes were dry, and my thirst was quenched.

Wiping the mud from my arms with Its hands, The Figure asked me, "Do you remember what you did on June 25th, 25 years ago?"

I had to think about it. That was the summer before I turned 14, before I entered high school. I remembered being lonely around that time. I didn't have friends. No one really knew me.

"You knew Me then," The Figure reminded me.

"How did I know You?" I asked.

"Do you remember watching the sunset every night from the rocking chair in the living room?"

I remembered that, when I was 13, I did not fit in to what I was supposed to be at school. I was not interested in the things that people my age were interested in at that time. I didn't want to be part of either sitting around talking about others' faults or talking about boys, or worse than that (in my mind), do more than *talk* with boys. Boys didn't notice me anyway. I was not the quintessential beauty. On top of that, I was not a "good student." I got bored if I knew that what I was asked to do had no life-changing meaning for me. Since I didn't have friends to spend time with and didn't care about homework, I spent my time sitting in the living room every evening and listening to songs while watching the sunset. I was alone, but I was content.

"You weren't alone, Anna," The Figure told me. "I AM always with you. I AM with you even back in the living room."

"How? That isn't even grammatically possible."

"Do you remember when I told you that you do not know everything about who I AM?"

"Yes."

"Don't you have a deep desire to be known for who you

117

are?"

I thought about what The Figure asked and replied, "Most of my life, that has been my deepest desire. I want to be known, to be accepted, and to be loved for who I really am."

"Anna, this craving for needing to be known comes from a very sacred and special place. Why do you think I built *The Door*? Why do you think I came here to reveal who I AM to you and everyone else in the forest? We are *all* connected: our desires, our experiences, our consequences are all connected. What happened to Me affects you and what happens to you affects Me. What you do affects all the people who were trapped in The Mere Ore forest and what they do affects you. When people begin to realize that the Source of quenching all thirst for desire is Love – unmasked, unselfish, unconditional Love- they stop acting out of neglect and begin to nourish each other. You have deep cravings and thirst because you have been neglected; not by me or anyone in the forest, but by yourself. You ran away from the very things that could have quenched your thirst because you were scared that those things would leave you thirstier. That type of thinking is backwards from how you were designed, and this journey helped you unshackle, turn around, and make progress toward what you *really* desire. There is A Way to never thirst again. If you want Me to show you, I will."

"That is my desire."

"Then, are you ready to walk with Me through *The Door* and rebuild The Well?"

Every time that I was led to a new place in the forest, I had a battle to fight. I did not want to move anymore. I just wanted to sit there and talk to The Figure. Even though I felt stronger, I was still tired of fighting.

"I am covered in the mud of The Swamp," I said, making excuses to The Figure.

"Come with Me." The Figure got up and walked to the edge of The Swamp.

"I don't want to go anywhere near there."

"Do you *trust* Me?"

There was that word again.

"I keep thinking I do, but when You actually ask me to do something, I realize that I am still unsure."

"Well, we are about to find out," The Figure smiled confidently and commanded, "Submerge yourself in this water seven times."

"What? I just told you that I was tired and dirty. What part of doing that is going to help me?" This command was inconceivable to me.

"Do you *trust* Me?" The Figure emphasized The Word again.

"You keep on saying *that* word."

"I want you to *know* what it means."

"What will happen to me if I don't do it?"

"You'll see."

"Why can't you just tell me?"

"I *can* tell you, but *trust* requires not knowing the possible outcomes."

I knew that what The Figure said was right. I just didn't want to do what It asked me to do. I tried to negotiate my way out of going back in The Swamp.

Faith ran up to me, still in her child-like state. She was pulling her mother by the hand. In the most maturely grown-up voice coming from such a fragile little body, she encouraged me. "Anna, you can do this. Has The Figure ever done or said

119

anything that wasn't true?"

Her question caused me to reflect on all the times I spent with The Figure. I remembered the things we talked about, the ideas It taught me, and the way that It was always there when I needed help and when I celebrated victories. I thought about *The Door* containing The Figure's story. I realized that I had been asked to do stranger things than dip myself in a dirty swamp (while I was already dirty) in order to become clean. I understood that, if I was going to genuinely *trust*, I needed to *do* what The Figure asked of me, even when the commands did not make sense to me.

I knelt to meet Faith's face, whispered "Thank you," gave her a kiss on the cheek, stood back up, looked Fear in the eyes, and then turned around and walked toward The Figure.

Entering The Swamp, I could feel the mud squeeze my feet as each one hit the bottom of the surface's edge. I could feel the granules of sand exfoliating my feet and legs as I got in deeper. I could feel that I was being embraced by the dirt around me. My arms and hands stayed above the surface as my torso was submerged.

"Do I need to go all the way in?" I asked, trying to only do the bare minimum of requirements.

"What do you think?"

I sassily rolled my eyes, and The Figure looked at me like a teacher would look at a student who just asked if they actually had to do their homework. Of course, it was my choice: that bittersweet gift.

I submerged myself all the way.

One.

I came up as far as I could, took a breath, and then

submerged myself the second, third, and fourth time. Each time became more difficult. I wanted to give up.

Five.

Through my blurred eyes, I could see that, each time I went in and came back up, Faith grew as she stood on the shore. She transformed into a teenager. Fear still held her hand.

Six.

I came up out of the murky water the sixth time and saw that Hope and Acceptance joined Faith and Fear.

"One more time, Anna."

An Idle suddenly emerged and whispered a "What If." I contemplated it for a moment. Then, I took my necklace in my hand. I felt the thorns from the crown and showed it to the Idle, who quickly disappeared into the mud.

After taking a deep breath, I closed my eyes and went back down under the thick, murky water. I felt like I was slowly sinking into a lake of sap.

Seven.

When I came up that time, I noticed all the dirt was washed off me, and I was treading in a beautiful, freshwater lake. Instead of wondering how it was possible, I looked at Acceptance and decided to just enjoy what I had around me.

I invited the water to run across my skin and through my hair. When I finally swam back and stood on the edge of the former swamp (now called The Clear Sea), I noticed that my feet were free from splinters. I finally felt cleansed.

On the shore, I was greeted by Acceptance, Hope, Fear, The Figure, and Faith, who had grown into a woman again.

"Do you remember about June 25th now?" asked The Figure.

I did. I remembered being submerged in water that day. I remembered that I chose The Figure publically for the first time that day. It took 25 years to *genuinely* choose and trust The Figure.

"I am going to prepare a place for you to rest, Anna," said The Figure, knowing what I needed. "I will meet you at *The Door.*" Faith and Fear followed The Figure.

Acceptance, Hope, and I traveled together through the forest for a few weeks. We looked at the trees and all their variety. Each one had its own beauty. I felt awakened to the idea that *this* is how people should be viewed. Even though we are all in the same place, we bring beauty through our uniqueness. I finally appreciated myself for the quirky, rare beauty I brought to the forest. Acceptance wrapped her arms around my shoulders. I really enjoyed the times when we embraced each other.

I looked at the path under my newly revived feet. I could feel affection from the ground seeping into my soles. I welcomed it with each step. Hope looked at me and smiled.

When we arrived at *The Door*, The Figure was not there.

"Where is The Figure?" I asked.

"You'll see," assured Acceptance, and I knew what that phrase meant now. I needed to *trust.*

"Look, Anna. What do you see in *The Door* now?" Wisdom asked.

I looked at *The Door* again. This time, I could see more of my story interwoven in the stories of the panels.

"I see myself in *The Door,*" I replied. I saw myself at The Tree and The Well in the 1st panel. I also saw myself at The Well in the 4th section of the 43rd panel. I saw myself standing at the foot of the chopped down and re-constructed tree that appeared at the end of the 40th, 41st, 42nd, and 43rd panels.

"Anna, every time you come to *The Door*, it will reveal new understandings for you," said Wisdom. She took a splinter from *The Door* and put it into one of the last empty spaces on my necklace.

"Look at the necklace now," I said as I showed her the shattered pieces of glass from the Mere Ore forest, the thorns from the crown, the pen that I used to pic gratitude on the walls of The Secret Cave, and the jewels that all the Secrets gave to me all surrounded by the original pearls, sapphires, and graphite. "It is complete now," I said, not seeing any voided spaces to place any more treasures.

"Almost," said Wisdom.

"What else is there?" I asked.

"You still have to ask? Anna, what has been the desire of your heart while you have been here in the forest?"

I thought about Wisdom's question. What was my heart's desire? Sometimes, I forget I even have a heart. Sometimes, my heart feels like it is trapped.

"I don't know. I feel like I have been running around the forest seeking my desire, but I don't really know what I am looking for in the end."

"Maybe it is time to ask yourself what it is you want and then seek it until you find it," suggested Wisdom.

I thought about Wisdom's suggestion. The first step to having the desires of my heart is to know what they are. I wouldn't be able to recognize them if I didn't know what I was looking for in the first place. The first step is to ask.

"How will I know the desires of my heart?"

"You need to find your heart and ask it," said Wisdom.

"Isn't my heart with me right now?"

"Anna, your heart is waiting for you beyond *The Door*."

"Beyond *The Door*?" I asked, seeking understanding. "How? Where? Why is my heart not with me?"

"It is trapped under a pile of crumbled rubble, and only you can lift the stones that will set it free," Wisdom informed me.

"Is that why I have felt a void since The Well crumbled?" I asked.

"Anna, the purpose of your journey since The Well crumbled was to save and heal your heart," Wisdom replied. "You just didn't have the strength that you needed until now."

"Are you ready to see what is on the Other Side of *The Door*?" Hope appeared and asked.

I was reassured to know that Hope was with me. However, her question baffled me. The Other Side of *The Door*? I knew that *The Door* was *a door,* but I never thought about it leading *Somewhere.* All this time, I just thought of *The Door* the way I thought of a statue. It just stood in the middle of the forest as something to contemplate. I didn't think of it having a function.

"Go ahead, Anna," said Acceptance.

"What am I supposed to do?" I asked.

"What do you think you are supposed to do when you want a door to open?" she responded.

"Close a window?" I jokingly bantered. We all laughed.

I stepped up to *The Door,* admired the craftsmanship that The Figure put into the details. I loved seeing the stories that came to life on the panels. I looked around for The Figure, who was nowhere to be seen. It was supposed to be there. It said it would. It never broke Its Word to me before.

I hesitated, hoping that The Figure would surprise me and magically appear. Hope nodded at me in encouragement. I finally raised my hand to knock at *The Door*, when I heard a knock coming from The Other Side.

I looked at Acceptance, who just shrugged her shoulders and smiled.

"What do I do?" I asked.

"Open *The Door*, Anna," commanded Hope.

When I opened *The Door*, I saw a man dressed in princely garments. I felt like I needed to bow or kneel, as He gestured His arm to welcome me to The Other Side of *The Door*. This was a significant moment, and I couldn't help but continue to wonder where The Figure was. Why, at this moment, The Figure would be somewhere else nagged at me.

"Excuse me," I didn't know what to call The Man. "Sire, I mean, Your Highness…"

I was interrupted by The Man when He whispered, "Anna," while extending two wounded hands.

I knew that voice. I knew those hands. The One in front of me was The Figure, transfigured.

"It's You," came out of my mouth. "You are…"

"Yes, I know. You are finally able to see me beyond *The Door*, Anna. Your perspective is different. I am not impersonal to you anymore. You can see me for what I AM here on this Side of *The Door*. In order for Me to go into the forest and share about who I AM, this is what I had to become. Very few people in the forest were able to see Me for who I AM before that; others still see Me the way that you saw Me before you opened *The Door*: a helpful, friendly *being* that they could never *figure* out. I became human when I came into the forest over 2000 years ago so that people could relate to Me because I related to them first. I was homeless; I was ridiculed; I was beaten to death. I wanted the people in the forest to know that, not only do I understand their pain, but I *chose* to go through this pain to show them how much I love them. When people seek Me in and beyond *The Door*, they will see Me for who I truly AM."

"Go *figure!*" I chuckled. Then, I became serious. "I want to know You more."

"Anna, from the beginning of this story, you listened to what I told you to do because you saw what I was capable of doing, and you eventually *trusted* that. By opening *The Door*, you chose to see Me in a different Light. You *trust* My Story, you see yourself as part of My Story, and you chose a relationship with Me. It is inevitable that you see Me this way. On this Side of *The Door*, you are in My Kingdom. I left this Place to enter into My Story because I wanted to show the people in the forest how much I want them to open T*he Door* and come *Here*," He said pointing at all of the beautiful sights around us, "and *trust* that I would do anything truly good for them because of how much I love them."

I wanted to scream out, "I love You!" to The Figure, but, as if He could read my mind, He interrupted my intended action with, "*Saying* 'I love You,'" The Figure paused with a smirk, " is not what I want to *hear* from you."

It took me a split second before I realized what The Figure was trying to tell me.

"What *more* do You want then?" I joined into the playfulness as I inquired.

"Don't *talk* of stars or rain or Fall, Anna."

"I understand," I could barely get the words out without

being overcome with laughter. At that moment, I realized that I reached a deep level of intimacy The Figure. Now, it was time for me to act accordingly.

"Are you ready to follow Me?" The Figure asked.

"Ready? Now? I've *been* following You, haven't I?"

"Well," The Figure paused, "This time, it will be different."

"How so?"

The Figure looked ahead of us on the path beyond *The Door* and whispered, "You'll see," with a smile.

"You keep using that phrase. I'm starting to understand what it means," I responded, joining in with His playfulness.

"Walk this way with Me," The Figure commanded as He started to mirthfully march forward with sporadic jump-kicks.

I had only seen the playful side of The Figure a few times before. We usually acted so formal and serious. I liked experiencing Him this way too.

Marching forward, I chose to follow His lead. We walked through the forest together and laughed. Joy found us. Although she didn't say much, she walked with us and her presence invited us into giggling so much that we all fell over with side aches from laughter. When I looked up from where I fell to the ground, I realized that we were next to a giant rock.

The Figure put His hands on the giant rock, turned to me, took my hands in His, looked me in the eyes, and said, "I am bringing you back here soon, but you need to come with Me to one more place first." I wasn't scared of what awaited me at the next place. I used to be scared, but since I already experienced the teeter-totter of life's exchange between pleasant and difficult experiences with The Figure, I was comfortable in trusting His adventures.

We walked for a few days together before we arrived at the place where The Well once stood.

"After The Well crumbled, you had many questions. You pondered the Universe and its purpose. That is when I arrived," The Figure reminded me of the beginning of this journey. "If The Well didn't crumble, you would not have asked those important questions, and you might have missed out on this entire journey. You would have continued being distracted by Idles and would have continued to give Ego the power that you now have. All circumstances worked together for you to be here in this moment with Me."

"I wouldn't change any of it to trade what we have now."

"I'm glad," The Figure smiled. "It is time for you to set your heart free and rebuild The Well, Anna."

It Is Well

The Figure pointed to the pile of stones. "your heart is trapped under that pile."

All this time, I have been in the forest fighting for my heart, and it has been trapped under the debris of The Well that crumbled. "Wisdom told me that my heart was trapped under a pile of rubble. Why did I need to go all the way around the forest just to come back full circle to where I started?"

"Anna, as Wisdom also said, you were not strong enough to move the stones before. All of the battles you won gave you the strength you needed to lift these stones and free your heart."

I walked over to the pile of stones and lifted them, one by one, off each other. Some of the stones were heavier than others. Some had jagged edges that made it difficult to pick them up without piercing my skin. I was familiar with being wounded that way, so when I was occasionally jabbed by the rougher stones, I simply took care of my needs and then kept lifting.

The trees around me were quietly watching this time. They were no longer threatening. Their leaves waved at me as they rustled in the wind, making a sound like a subtle applause. Their cheering summoned Hope. She stood next to The Figure and watched as I finished lifting the last stone off the dry hole in the ground where The Well once stood. At the bottom of the hole, I saw a little bird covered in dust; its wings matted down from being pressed under the stones.

I looked at The Figure and asked, "Is that little bird my heart?"

"Yes," was all that The Figure said in reply, as He put His

arm around Hope and waited for me to rescue the little bird.

"Oh! You poor thing! Look at you," I whispered as tears once again began to well up in my eyes. "You are so fragile, weak, and wounded," I said, scooping up the little bird from its potential grave. It struggled to take breaths and flutter its broken wings. It was alive, but it needed to heal. "I need to protect you now. I do not want anything to happen to you again."

"Anna, there is only one way to protect it that will guarantee that it won't get hurt again," Wisdom appeared and warned.

"You can hide it and never let it fly freely or land on someone's shoulder to sing its sweet song in their ears," said Fear.

"Or you can give it to The Figure, and it *will* be able to fly freely," said Wisdom.

I held my heart in my hands, not wanting to ever let it go. I wanted to protect it. "What if I just put it in a cage? I can still hear it sing. I don't ever want it out of my sight again."

"Why don't you carve a cage out of The Rock you found with Joy?" Fear suggested.

I liked that idea. "Can You bring me back to The Rock?" I asked The Figure, who nodded and stood in place for a while before He began walking in the direction of The Rock. The Emotions followed behind us

Once we got there, I looked at the massive heap of stone in front of me. There was so much potential for this to become a solid cage for my heart. "How am I going to make a cage out of this?" I asked The Emotions.

"You know, your necklace is not just a reminder of where you have been and what you have learned; it contains tools that you can use to help you beyond the journey you went on to acquire all of them," Wisdom enlightened me as she walked over to me and held onto the pen from the necklace in her right hand. "You used this to break down the walls of The Secret Cave."

"You can use it to carve a cage for Your Heart," Fear suggested.

"Well, that is one thing she can do," Wisdom said in a somewhat solemn tone.

"Where can I put my heart while I make a cage for it?" I asked.

Wisdom, Fear, and Hope all looked at The Figure, who held out His wounded hands, inviting me to trust Him with my heart.

I took my heart and handed it to The Figure. As if it recognized Him, my heart snuggled into His wounded hands; its wings fluttered.

Feeling like my heart was in Good Hands, I took the pen from my necklace and began to write on The Rock. As I penned, little pieces of stone started to fall away. I wrote about crossing The Swamp. I wrote about *The Door* having another Side, and how The Figure was so much more personal on the Other Side of it. I wrote about lifting the remains of The Well and finding my heart. Each memory and experience that I wrote about created intricate details in The Rock. After a few days, The Cage for my heart was finished.

"Where is my heart? I made a safe place for it to stay," I asked The Figure.

"Look," The Figure said, pointing at the sky. My heart was trying to fly again.

"No! Don't let it do that! It might get hurt!" I said, frustrated at The Figure for letting my heart explore.

"It is not unsafe, Anna," The Figure reassured me. I have

had My eye on it the whole time. He whistled to the bird, and it flew down to His hands. "Here," The Figure extended His hand to give me back the little bird. Once it was back in my hands, He asked, "What are you going to name it?"

I looked at the little bird in my hand. "I am just going to name it what it is. Hello, Sparrow," I said to my heart.

"That is a beautifully appropriate name," Acceptance acknowledged.

"I know you are still sick, and I know that you need time to heal. I made a cage for you, so no one can hurt you again," I told Sparrow, as I placed it in The Cage.

"It is going to love this protective place you made, Anna," Fear reassured me as Sparrow jumped around safely in its cage.

Over the course of a few weeks, it became stronger. Sometimes, it popped its little head between the stone bars of The Cage and sang. The melody of the song seemed sad. I wondered what it could possibly be sad about now that it was safe.

"Have you ever considered letting Sparrow out of The Cage to fly around?" Hope asked.

"It needs to get well before it can fly again," Fear told Hope.

"How will we know when it is well?" I asked.

"It will *always* be susceptible to the dangers of the forest, Anna," said The Figure. "Of course, The Cage will keep it safe from those dangers, but Sparrow was not made to be in a cage."

"What do You suggest I do, let it fly around freely again? After what it has been through?" I didn't really want to hear the answer; I already knew what The Figure was going to suggest.

"Do you *trust* Me?"

After all I have been through with The Figure, He still asked me that question again, and I still struggled with genuinely saying yes.

"It has been put in others' hands before and has been so damaged from Ego and Carelessness. I am still so tired and slightly wounded from cleaning up the mess of the crumbled well. I just don't know if I could ever go through this type of journey to free it again if something happens to it."

"Let Me take care of it then, Anna. You can to choose to let it be in My care. Once you do, you can be assured that it will be able to fly around safely. I AM the only One who can keep that promise to you, Anna."

"Yes, Anna! Let Him take care of Sparrow!" Hope reaffirmed.

I looked over at Fear, who nodded at me in approval as she was wrapped in the arms of her grown-up daughter. They were such a beautiful pair at that moment. Faith's features were so defined and mature, it was hard to believe she was ever so small and helpless. Even though she had visibly grown up, she still had a child-like sparkle in her eyes. When Faith looked at me with those eyes, she reminded me that she had grown because of the experiences I had on my journey with The Figure. I knew that I needed to continue to act in accordance with trusting Him.

"It's time," Wisdom said.

I knew she was right. I went to The Cage and held out my hand for Sparrow. It tilted its head to the side inquisitively, and I motioned my fingers for it to come to me. It cautiously hopped into my hand, and I lifted it carefully out of The Cage.

"I *trust* You," I said to The Figure as I handed Sparrow to Him.

"I'll keep My eye on you, Sparrow," The Figure smiled as one eye was open and the other winked closed.

Sparrow sang a little tune in reply. The Figure lifted His hands and Sparrow began to fly freely. It sang the tune again as it flew around, stronger than ever.

"Now, it sings because it's happy," I said, noticing the tune was different from the one I heard when it was in The Cage.

"It sings because it's free," said The Figure.

We laughed together, as we knew exactly what we were communicating to each other with those words. They were the lyrics to Sparrow's song.

"That song was well-written, wasn't it?" The Figure smiled at me when He jokingly asked.

"Well," I said, continuing to play with words, "if I made a wish, it would be that everyone would be able to experience this type of journey."

"Well," The Figure continued the banter, "why don't you write about it? You have a pen. Put it to use, Anna."

"I thought You said it was time for me to rest now?"

"Anna, this will bring you rest. *Trust* Me," The Figure looked up at Sparrow, flying around happily and freely, singing its joyful song with 'birds of a feather' flying around and singing with it. "Do you remember when you questioned the why's and how's of the Universe?"

"Yes, right before I saw You after The Well crumbled."

"Well," another smile beamed from His princely face, "do you remember when you figured out that Uni is One and verse is a written passage or a part of a song and that this journey you have been on is just One verse in My Story and My Song? It is time for you to write this down so that others can hear your part of My Song and know that we are all part of the same Song. Knowing that we are all, in our own unique way, connected and living accordingly *is* the purpose of the Uni-verse. You can create your part of My Song for others to observe the way that they look at My Story on *The Door.*"

The Figure's words inspired me to continue to write. I took the pen from my necklace and began to carve on The Cage around the bars. I kept writing until The Cage took a different form.

The process was not as easy or quick as I thought it would be. There were times when I got distracted by the noises of the forest and times when I needed to rest. I walked to *The Door* many times to be inspired. I went to The Secret Cave to remind myself of the beauty that shines Inside.

I wrote so much for so long that I thought it would never be finished, but, one day, I stood back and looked at the work that I did, and I knew that The Rock was carved into what it was supposed to become in the first place.

"Maktub," I said to the air around me. I finally had it written, chiseled in stone with the pen. This specific journey was recorded to be shared. I could not wait to celebrate its completion, so I went to The Court Yard to gather everyone.

"Wisdom, Hope, Acceptance, Fear, Faith!" I called.

They all rushed to me. Hope and Acceptance followed Faith and her mother. They were all dressed like bridesmaids, each in unique styles of purple colored dresses. They each had a bouquet of amaryllis, delphinium, freesia, orchids and irises. The flowers were more vibrant than I remembered from the last time I was at The Court Yard.

I heard a murmuring off in the distance. It sounded different than the noises I heard the first time I arrived. "What is that?" I asked.

"Come and see," Hope said.

We all walked to The Table in The Court Yard. I went there to surprise them, but they all surprised me instead! I was shocked to see all the people from The Mere Ore Forest sitting with The Secrets at The Table.

"We are all gathered here today to celebrate you, Anna," Faith proclaimed. "This journey has brought you through many difficult battles and many victories. We know that it seemed like the battles would never end. There will be more for you to face, but those battles will not be quite like the ones you have been through on this journey. You have worked hard to free your heart, and it is time for you to enjoy the fruits of your labor," Faith pointed to The Table covered in ripe produce. "After you freed the people in The Mere Ore Forest and The Secrets, they came here immediately to help us prepare this special event for you. We are all so happy to be here with you to celebrate!"

I couldn't believe that everyone who had taken part in my journey was there! I looked at the faces of people from The Mere Ore Forest sitting across from Forgiveness. The Secrets were seated around Acceptance. Anger and Shame were not invited.

After surveying my supportive guests, I noticed how beautiful The Table was covered in shiny linens, crystal dishes, flower-arrangements, candles, and platters full of fruit. It looked like a wedding feast!

"Where is The Figure?" I asked.

"Here I AM," He said as He called to me from the Other Side of The Table, looking more gloriously handsome than ever! He walked up to me, invited my hands into His, looked me in the eyes, and smiled. His eyes were full of something I *still* had to figure out.

"There is someone else we want you to meet," Hope said, interrupting the glances that The Figure and I exchanged.

"She has been sleeping for a long time, and she is so excited to finally see you again!" said Faith.

"Hello, Anna!" said Love, who was finally awake. She was wearing a flowing, ivory dress and carrying lilacs. "I feel like I have missed so much! We have quite a bit of catching up to do, don't we?" She took one of my hands in hers, leaving the other in The Figure's, and whispered, "We have a beautiful adventure awaiting us! I'm glad that I am *well-rested.*"

"You are absolutely stunning!" I told Love. I couldn't take my eyes off her.

"It has taken a while for me to become this way, Anna. Ego had me as her prisoner and cast a spell on me to fall asleep, so that she could protect you and make you into what she wanted you to be. She knew that if I am awake, you are content, and she cannot control you. My sleeping spell could only be broken when you let your heart fly freely."

"Well," I said, pausing to let the word ring in their ears, "Sparrow is flying freely and The Cage that I originally made for it is gone. There is something that I want everyone to see," I told her, even though I had a feeling she already knew.

I summoned everyone to get up from The Table and walk with me to place where The Cage used to be. Sparrow was flying above, watching all of us. It was singing a new song.

Once we arrived, I turned to all who were around me and shared, "I began this journey when The Well crumbled and my heart was trapped. It has been an adventure meeting all of you and having your support while I built strength to lift the stones to free my heart," I paused and looked at Forgiveness, Wisdom, Acceptance, Faith, Hope, Love, and even Fear, with their long, purple dresses flowing in the wind. "I thought that I was supposed to build The Cage for my heart so that it would not be harmed anymore, but when I gave my heart to The Figure and He let it fly, I knew what The Rock was really meant to be. I have been carving this with my pen for a long time, and I am ready to share it with all of you." I uncovered my masterpiece.

"Welcome to Sparrow's Well." I lowered a bucket into the opening and pulled it back up. The water in the bucket sparkled, and I poured some into my cup. I handed the overflowing cup to Love. "Go ahead," I told her, and she took a sip. "I want this to be yours, Love. I want you to share it with everyone who passes this way. When people come here to the place I carved with the pen, I want you to give them a drink and tell them about what it took to rebuild The Well and to wake you up."

"As you wish, Anna," Love replied.

I turned to The Figure and asked, "I *trust* You to help me maintain Sparrow's Well. I cannot do it on my own. I have already tried to maintain it on my own once, and it dried up and crumbled. I need You. I know The Antagonist is going to try to destroy this one the way the other one was destroyed. Please, help me keep Sparrow's Well sturdy and clean, so others in the forest can come here and have their thirst quenched when they are on their own journey. I know that just because this part of my journey in the Uni-Verse has come to an end, it is the beginning of a new one. I learned that from You. I have learned so much from You, and now I want to put that into practice. You gave me this gift," I lifted the pen from my necklace, "and because of

138

what I have learned and seen at *The Door* and on this journey with You, I will continue to use it for the purpose that You intended."

The Figure turned to me and smiled. He lifted one of his wounded hands up to put one of Sparrow's feathers in my necklace. "It is complete now, Anna." Then, He opened His arms into an inviting embrace, and proclaimed, "Well done."

Sparrow's Well

Afterward

Sharing the journey that I went on to mend my broken heart required a vulnerability that liberated and terrified me all at the same time. While writing this story, I had to dig deeply to find the roots of the obstacles that kept me from freeing my heart awakening genuine Love. As I typed, I felt myself confronting my actual emotions and demons (sometimes one and the same) while changing the course of their power and influence on me.

Most of the intricacies and symbols came to me sporadically. I jotted them down in my daily journal, in between the epiphanies and goals of my "other" daily life. Sometimes, they appeared as I typed, reinforcing my belief that my story is connected to something bigger than myself.

What was even more serendipitous was when I began to see parts of my story in television shows, songs, sermons, vacation experiences, restaurant decor, and conversations that I had with people. Even after I had already written the words, and they came to life in my off-the-page world.

The purpose for writing this story was not motivated by being recognized for any literary accomplishment. Obviously, that would be The Queen's plan. I do not consider myself to be an author. I am simply the storyteller of my own experience: working through my broken heart and building a healthy relationship with myself, so that I can create more meaningful experiences while I am still alive in this realm of existence.

I wrote this story to heal. Publishing this fantastical memoir is simply an extension of my healing. Being vulnerable enough to share my journey has hopefully inspired you to begin or continue your own journey into *your* Mere Ore Forest, Secret Cave, and Swamp. I hope it has inspired to you to discover new perspectives for how to interpret *The Door* and find treasures to build something that will quench your thirst and, in return, inspire others when you share during a feast at your Court Yard Table. Then, enjoy the thirst-quenching experience that comes from your own heart's Living Well.

Acknowledgements

While the plot, conflict, and theme manifested from my own journey, I attribute much of the inspiration to a few family members, friends, and authors who, by sharing their insights with me, sparked ideas for the symbolism, setting and characters' names.

The Bible, being *The Door,* was a major contributor to the ideas that blossomed in this story.

C.S. Lewis inspired so much of my understanding of The Figure and of the magic we can find in the forest. His works reveal many symbolic mysteries in this world.

William Goldman's *The Princess Bride* inspired some of the settings, as well as much the witty banter and some of the quotes of some of the characters.

John Bunyan's *Pilgrim's Progress* inspired me to name my characters who they were.

John and Stasi Eldredge's *Captivating* was a beautiful source of inspiration for many ideas of how to heal my heart, in addition to understanding the meaning of the word *Ezer.*

Paulo Coelho's *The Alchemist* taught me to read and heed the omens in life, as well as about the word, "maktub."

Brene Brown's *The Gifts of Imperfection* led me to understand Shame and gave inspiration for the stained-glass art in The Secret Cave.

My Mama, for her example, experience, and insight that have been my road-signs on this journey to heal my heart and know that it needs to be in The Figure's hands and for being the first person read this all the way through.

My Papa, for encouraging me when I edited the final version of this story and for continued support that makes it possible for me to pursue my purpose.

Lisa, for unconditional love and amazing photography skills.

John and Melissa, for discussing and revealing characteristics of The Figure to me and for Melissa's editing help and reading Proverbs together- one chapter every day so we could have the combined epiphany that Pro-verb meant "The Word in action."

Sara, for her hospitality, rainy day couch conversation, and editing some of the first parts of this book.

Dr. Joe, for his encouragement and being willing to read the first few chapters for clarity.

Dan, for his editing help, author advice, and inspiration to let this book be what it is going to be.

Deb, for her friendship and willingness to spend 3 hours on a Sunday to help me know where to begin editing and for still being so supportive after reviewing the most confusing versions of Chapter 1-3.

Danny, for listening to the first unedited audio version attempt and for helping me realize that pencils are made of graphite.

Chris, for the approximately 3 million minutes devoted to editing and discussing and creating crowning achievements, for his devotion and attention during the final days of editing, and for inspiring me to practice what I have learned from my journey.

Violeta, for her intuitive perfection in creating a cover that encompasses the motifs of this story.

Ray, for his patience with my perfectionism and assistance in making sure my story is shared with those who so choose to find it on the platforms that he set up for me.

About the Storyteller

Anna Marie Savino has always loved writing and sharing her passion for making meaningful connections between words and ideas. The two interests fused together in *Sparrow's Well*, her first published book.

More of her writing can be found on her website and in *Fueled by Coffee and Love: A Brew Perspective*, (in addition to a giant bin that contains years' worth of journal writing and notebooks from high school).

Although not a writer by trade, after 16 years of teaching English to high-school and junior-high students, she decided to practice what she preaches and be a model of how narrative can positively change lives.

www.wellculturedperspectives.com

@sparrow_well

@sparrowswellbook

wellculturedperspectives@gmail.com